"I have only myself to offer."

Mikayla hurriedly sought to clarify. "As your mistress. Sexually, socially, for a year."

Rafael had a desire to shake her, and didn't stop to query *why*. "That's the deal?"

His voice was dangerously quiet, and Mikayla barely suppressed a shiver of apprehension. Would he take it?

"I'm prepared to negotiate."

HELEN BIANCHIN was born in New Zealand and traveled to Australia before marrying her Italian-born husband. After three years they moved, returned to New Zealand with their daughter, had two sons then resettled in Australia. Encouraged by friends to recount anecdotes of her years as a tobacco sharefarmer's wife living in an Italian community, Helen began setting words on paper and her first novel was published in 1975. An animal lover, she says her terrier and new Persian kitten regard her study as being as much theirs as hers.

Look out for *The Husband Test* (#2218)
by Helen Bianchin
in Presents Passion
on-sale December 2001

Helen Bianchin

MISTRESS BY CONTRACT

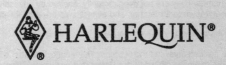

HARLEQUIN®

TORONTO • NEW YORK • LONDON
AMSTERDAM • PARIS • SYDNEY • HAMBURG
STOCKHOLM • ATHENS • TOKYO • MILAN • MADRID
PRAGUE • WARSAW • BUDAPEST • AUCKLAND

ISBN 0-373-12201-2

MISTRESS BY CONTRACT

First North American Publication 2001.

Copyright © 2001 by Helen Bianchin.

Visit us at www.eHarlequin.com

Printed in U.S.A.

CHAPTER ONE

THE sun shone warmly, Rafael noted as he spared a glance out of the kitchen window while water poured into the glass carafe. With deft movements he turned off the tap and slid the carafe onto the coffee-maker, spooned freshly ground coffee beans into the filter, then switched it on.

The eggs were done, the toast ready, and on impulse he placed it all on a tray and carried it out onto the terrace.

He returned to the kitchen, all but drained the orange juice in a few long swallows, then he poured the coffee, collected the morning newspaper, and ventured into the early Spring sunshine.

Allowing himself time for a leisurely breakfast had long become a habit, and this morning was no different.

Best part of the day, he reflected with satisfaction as he skimmed the headlines, read what interested him, whilst enjoying the food he'd prepared.

He perused the business section, then reached the social pages, scanned the photo spread and was in the process of turning the page when his own image leapt out in a lower right corner frame.

Hmn, Sasha looked stunning. The profile was perfect, the smile just right, her stance practised to present the most attractive image.

His gaze slid to the caption, and his eyes narrowed a little.

Celebrating the recent takeover by Aguilera, Rafael Velez-Aguilera, multi-millionaire entrepreneur, and Sasha Despojoa enjoy an evening at Déjeuner restaurant.

A brooding smile barely moved his mobile mouth.

Yes, he could lay claim to wealth and business nous, he reflected with grim satisfaction. He lived in a beautiful home in one of Sydney's prestigious harbour suburbs. He possessed an enviable investment portfolio, and owned real estate in several capital cities.

It would appear he had it all.

What the columnist didn't touch on was his background.

The backstreet poverty in which he'd been raised, the less than salubrious place of education where the tough survived and the meek were discarded.

For as long as he could remember he'd wanted more than just an existence on the wrong side of town. More than a life having to keep an eye on the lookout for whoever walked the law enforcement beat, the necessity to always be one step ahead, glib words at the ready to slip from a practised tongue. There wasn't a thing he hadn't witnessed, few deals he hadn't done.

From a young age he'd wanted out. Out of the grey world where survival was the only ambition. Being street-smart was only part of the goal. Education was the other, and he'd fought for it the only way he knew how, gaining scholarships and graduating with honours. Not for the glory or honour, not to please his parents. For himself.

He'd succeeded handsomely. At thirty-six, he was precisely where he wanted to be. He could have any woman he wanted, and frequently did, selectively.

His latest companion, however, was hinting at permanence and, while he enjoyed her in bed, out of it he had no desire to commit to a lasting relationship.

Was there any *one* woman for a man? The *only* one.

Somehow he doubted it.

The shrill peal of the mobile phone intruded, and he picked up and intoned a brusque greeting. 'Velez-Aguilera.'

'Buenos dias, querido.'

The feminine voice was a sultry purr, and intentionally feline. It was meant to quicken his heartbeat and stir his loins in a reminder of what he'd chosen not to accept the previous night. 'Sasha,' he acknowledged.

'Am I disturbing you, darling?'

A double entendre, if ever there was one. 'No,' he responded truthfully.

'I thought we might have dinner tonight.'

He appreciated a woman's eagerness, but he preferred to do the hunting. 'I'll have to take a rain-check.'

'Some other time, then?'

She'd recovered quickly, but the need for reassurance was there, and he chose to ignore it. 'Perhaps.' And ended the call.

He cast a brooding gaze out over the immaculate grounds, skimmed the shimmering blue waters of the swimming pool, and lingered on the tennis court, the flower beds and shrubbery before returning his attention to the newspaper.

He poured a fresh cup of coffee, checked his watch, and spread marmalade conserve on the last piece of toast. Five minutes later he re-entered the kitchen, rinsed and stacked plates into the dishwasher, then went upstairs to dress.

He owned any number of business suits, and today he chose Armani, added a buttoned waistcoat, a silk tie, slid his feet into handmade Italian shoes, shrugged on the jacket, checked his wallet, his briefcase, caught up his laptop, then retraced his steps to the ground floor.

The security system set, he gained the garage, slid in behind the wheel of a sleek top-of-the-range Mercedes, and sent the vehicle purring down the driveway.

He owned office space on a high floor in one of the city's glass-panelled buildings, an architectural masterpiece commanding splendid views out over the city harbour.

Traffic was heavy, and he opened his laptop at a set of lights, checked his day's scheduled appointments, and made a quick note to have his secretary make two phone calls.

Fifteen minutes later he eased the car down two floors of the basement car park and slid into his reserved space.

With deft movements, he shut off the ignition, caught up the laptop, his briefcase, opened the door and slid to his feet.

'Rafael Velez-Aguilera.'

He stilled at the sound of the feminine voice, and turned slowly to face its owner, his body alert beneath its relaxed demeanour, ready to strike at the first sign of aggression.

Blonde, petite, slender, green eyes, attractive features. She didn't seem a likely opponent, but then looks didn't mean a thing. He was aware what a practised martial arts expert could do, and knew that size or gender wasn't a consideration.

Was she concealing a weapon? His gaze narrowed, noting the way her hands held her leather bag. If she had a knife or a gun in there, he could disarm her before she moved an inch.

Dammit, these floors, the entire building was patrolled by security. How did she get in?

'Yes.'

'I need to talk to you.'

He slanted an eyebrow and watched her carefully, assessing her next move.

'I'm a busy man.' With slow deliberation he pulled back the cuff of his jacket and checked his watch.

'Five minutes.' She'd practised the words, timed them, and could manage it in less, if she had to.

'Make an appointment with my secretary.' The dismissal was clear.

'I tried that.' She shook her head. Nothing depicted in the media could accurately portray the essence of the man, or convey his compelling aura of power.

'It didn't work.' She managed a tight smile. 'Your security is impenetrable.'

'You managed to access this car park.' He'd have someone on it immediately.

'Guile.' A desperate plea based on truth to the security guard. She could only hope it wouldn't mean his job.

Rafael had to hand it to her. She had guts. 'Which you now hope to use on me?'

'And waste more time?'

He was intrigued. 'Two minutes,' he stipulated. 'Your name?'

'Mikayla.' The next part, she knew, would have a damning effect. 'Joshua Petersen's daughter.'

His expression tightened, his mouth thinned, and his voice when he uttered the single negative was lethal. 'No.'

It was just as she'd expected, but she persisted. She *had* to. 'You offered me two minutes.'

'I could multiply it by ten, and the answer would still be no.'

'My father is dying,' she stated simply.

'You want my sympathy?'

'Leniency.'

His features hardened, and his gaze pierced hers, inflexible, dangerous. 'You would dare ask leniency for a man who embezzled several hundred thousand dollars from me?'

She tamped down the sheer desperation. 'My father is hospitalised with an inoperable brain tumour.' She waited a beat. 'If you press charges against him, he'll spend his last weeks on earth incarcerated in prison.'

'No.' He activated the car alarm, pocketed the keys, and began walking towards the lift bank.

'I'll do anything.' It was a desperate last-ditch attempt. Two hand-delivered letters had been ignored, and phone calls hadn't been returned.

He paused, turned, and raked her slender frame with insulting appraisal. 'It would take more...' He paused thoughtfully. 'Much more than you're capable of giving.'

'You don't know that.'

'Yes,' he drawled with certainty. 'I do.'

If he got into the key-operated lift, she'd lose him. 'Please.'

He heard the word, sensed the slight tremor in her voice, and kept walking. He summoned the lift, then turned.

'You have one minute to get out of this car park, or you'll be arrested for trespass.'

He expected anger, rage, even an attempt at attack. Or a well-acted bout of weeping.

Instead he saw pride in the tilt of that small feminine chin. Her mouth moved fractionally as she sought control, and momentarily lost as the faint shimmer of moisture dampened those sea-green eyes. A single tear escaped and ran slowly down one cheek.

An electronic beep announced the lift's arrival, and he used his key to open the doors, then he stepped into the cubicle and inserted the key into its slot.

His expression didn't change. 'Thirty seconds.' He turned the key, the doors slid closed, and he was transported swiftly to his suite of offices on a high floor.

He nodded briefly to the brunette manning the curved ultra-modern reception desk, offered a greeting to his secretary, and walked through to his office.

Electronic wizardry had earned him a fortune. Computer technology advanced at lightning speed, and the internet was his forte.

He flipped the intercom, confirmed the day's schedule with his secretary, and went to work.

Two hours later he saved the file he'd been working on, and summoned up the Petersen file.

Not that his memory needed refreshing. He'd travelled too many roads to be disturbed or haunted by anything. But a certain blonde female's features intruded, the image of that one solitary tear trickling down her cheek was there, a silent vulnerable entity, and he wanted it gone.

Joshua Petersen, widower, one child, Mikayla, single, twenty-five, teacher. It listed an address, telephone number, the school where she taught. Hobbies.

One eyebrow lifted. Tae-bo?

He scrolled down, printed out the information, folded the sheet and slid it into the inside pocket of his jacket.

Then he made a phone call. 'Get me everything you can on Joshua Petersen, medically, personally.'

The man had listed gambling debts as the reason for systematic financial fiddling. At the time Rafael hadn't delved deeper.

He had the answers an hour later. Medically, the facts Joshua Petersen's daughter had given checked out.

Rafael hit the print button, then re-read the message on hard copy.

There was proven fact the man had used the money to fund private hospital care for his wife stricken by a car accident and on life-support in a coma for months before she died.

His eyes skimmed to the date…six months ago.

The man had almost gotten away with it. Except an audit had picked up irregular deposits…his attempt at reparation. And his foray into gambling tabled a series of isolated incidents over a period of a month. A last-ditch attempt to recoup and repay?

Rafael leaned back in his chair, steepled his fingers and lowered his eyelids in thoughtful contemplation.

There was a fantastic panoramic view out over Sydney's inner harbour, a picture-book scene that temporarily escaped him.

What next?

Madre de Dios. What was he thinking? The father was a thief. Why should the daughter interest him?

Intrigue, he corrected later that afternoon. Human relationships, family loyalty. How far did hers extend?

He recalled the proud tilt of her chin, weighed it against the outward sign of emotion in that single escaping tear, and decided to find out.

Depressing the inter-office communication system, he contacted his secretary.

'If Mikayla Petersen calls, put her through.'

It took twenty-four hours, and he felt satisfaction at knowing he'd calculated correctly.

He kept it brief. 'Seven thirty.' He named a restaurant. 'Meet me there.'

Mikayla had schooled herself for another rejection, and for a brief moment she was torn between hope and despair.

'I can't.'

'Why not?'

She grimaced at the faint arrogance apparent. 'I work nights.'

'Call in sick.' His voice was silk-smooth and dangerous.

Dear heaven. She couldn't afford to lose her job. 'I finish at eleven,' Mikayla said steadily.

'Teaching duties?'

'Waiting tables.'

There was a moment's silence. 'Where?'

'Not your stamping ground,' she negated at once.

'Where?' He'd been in worse dives than she could imagine.

She told him.

'I'll be there.'

He was, slipping inside thirty minutes before closing time, and he sat at a table, ordered coffee, and observed the clientele, the way she handled them.

It made her nervous, as he'd intended it should. He watched the way she endeavoured to ignore him, and experienced wry amusement, only to have it change to mild irritation when a diner who'd imbibed too well ran his hand over her slenderly curved rear.

He didn't need to hear what she said, the message was plain. Her eyes held a dangerous sparkle, and there was a tinge of pink colouring her cheeks.

Did she resent the need that made her take a second job, as much as she resented her father for an act that inadvertently put her in this position?

Perhaps not. She had shown courage and pride. Qualities he identified with and admired. Wasn't that why he was here tonight?

At eleven Mikayla took a pile of dishes through to the kitchen, muttered a brief apology that she couldn't stay over time, then she untied and hung up her apron, quickly repaired her make-up and smoothed a hand over her hair before re-entering the restaurant.

Rafael Velez-Aguilera, Mikayla decided fleetingly, was not a man she could afford to keep waiting. He was standing at the door, and she moved out onto the pavement, and paused as he followed.

He extended an arm towards the opposite side of the road, and it took a few minutes to find a break in traffic.

The car was large and luxurious, the leather a rich texture beneath her fingers as she slid into the front seat.

He switched on the ignition, the engine purred into life, and he swung the vehicle out into the stream of cars heading into the city.

She didn't say a word. Coffee, he'd indicated. *Where* was hardly here nor there. Most certainly it wouldn't be in this area of town.

The silence bore heavily on her nerves. She had, for whatever reason, been given a chance. She dared not blow it.

It didn't take long to escape the less than salubrious inner city stretch where the night-life didn't cease until dawn, and enter the fringes of elite Double Bay where the beautiful people sipped espressos and lattes at pavement cafés and discussed past, present and future social events. Or criticised so-called friends and acquaintances.

There was, of course, a parking space just where he needed one, and she felt tension mount as he skilfully moved into it, then cut the engine.

How long would it take? She had assignments to mark for tomorrow's class. From school she'd gone straight to the hospital, then home in time to grab a bite to eat, change and present herself for work.

Dear heaven, her feet were killing her. The stiletto heels were part of the uniform; so were the sheer black hose, the short skirt, the skimpy top. She hated it almost as much as she hated the job.

She stood on the pavement, holding down the pain of aching calves, and forced herself to walk smoothly as he led her towards a trendy café.

He chose a pavement table, and they were no

sooner seated than a waiter appeared to take their order.

She requested a latte, decaffeinated or she'd never sleep, and felt her stomach swirl as he added a request for gourmet sandwiches.

'Eat,' Rafael commanded minutes later when the food arrived. He knew the scenario well. Food on the run, if she was lucky. Probably none.

He leaned back in his chair, watching her measured movements, the even white teeth as she took delicate bites, trying hard not to hurry and feed her hunger.

Rafael waited until she'd eaten two sandwiches, and sipped a third of her coffee, then he cut to the chase.

'I suggest you state your case,' he instructed silkily, and saw her hand pause momentarily, then she reset her cup onto the table.

Her hands retreated to her lap, where she clenched them together, hating Rafael Velez-Aguilera almost as much as she hated herself for the words she was about to say.

Her chin lifted, and her eyes deepened to emerald. 'I'm working two jobs, one of them seven nights a week. I also work weekends. Subtract rent, food, utilities, and it would take a lifetime to repay what my father owes you.' Oh, dear God, how did she suggest...? How *could* she? Dammit, she had no choice.

'I have only myself to offer.' This was the hardest thing she'd ever had to do, and she hurriedly sought to clarify. 'As your mistress. Sexually, socially, for a year.'

He had a desire to shake her, and didn't stop to query *why*. 'That's the deal?'

His voice was dangerously quiet, and she barely suppressed a shiver of apprehension. Would he take it? Dear Lord, what if he didn't?

'I'm prepared to negotiate.'

He surveyed her features with damning scrutiny, until she was close to screaming. 'On what terms?'

'I'll sign a pre-nuptial agreement stating I have no claim to any of your assets during our liaison, upon its conclusion or during my lifetime. In return, you waive any charges against my father.'

He took a moment to respond, and his voice assumed drawling cynicism. 'Such loyalty is admirable. But would you be prepared for the reality?'

She was dying inside, slowly. She forced herself to look at him, really look at him.

He was a large-framed man, tall, at least three or four inches over six feet. Dark, almost black hair. Superb facial bone structure, wide cheekbones, firm jaw, strong forehead. Piercing dark eyes, and a sensually moulded mouth.

There was something in his expression that bothered her. A hard ruthlessness that had little to do with astute business acumen. It went deeper than that. Beyond the expensive clothes, the visual trappings of success. He was, she deduced intuitively, a man who had seen much and weathered more.

It made him complex, dangerous. A quality that wasn't depicted in his biography, or apparent in any media photographs. Nor was it implicated by word, or visible in pictures among the social pages.

'I could be the lover from hell,' Rafael pursued silkily, and watched her expression freeze for an instant, then quickly recover.

'Or lousy in bed.'

His smile held wry amusement at her audacity.

Skilled, undoubtedly, she reflected with a degree of apprehension. He had the look, the self-assured knowledge of a man comfortable with himself and his expertise in being able to pleasure a woman.

How would she be able to go through with it? Sanity restored a sense of rationale. The chances of him agreeing to such a way-out proposal was almost nil.

Desperation shredded her nerves, and almost tore the breath from her throat.

There was nothing else. She'd sold her apartment, kept only the most basic furniture, downgraded her car, and emptied her bank account in a bid to help her father. It hadn't come close to covering a fraction of the debt he owed.

'You place a high price on your services.' He didn't relinquish his appraisal, and wondered if she knew how easy it was for him to read her.

To take payment in human kind wasn't new, Rafael mused. It went back centuries, and held many guises.

In today's society, it would be deemed coercion. Except it had been her suggestion, not his. Which placed a different complexion on the deal, and gave rise to the legalities of the situation.

It had intriguing connotations. No misconceptions, no false misunderstandings. It could even prove interesting.

Male satisfaction and gratification. Not the most enviable of reasons. Yet there was a part of him that wanted to have her beneath him, to drive her to the edge of sanity and hear her beg for release. Again and again.

Sexual chemistry, he attributed wryly, and wondered if he dare pursue it.

He watched as she ate the last sandwich and finished her coffee. The pallor had disappeared from her cheeks, also the sharp brightness from her eyes.

'More coffee?'

Mikayla pressed the paper napkin to her lips, then discarded it. She felt tired, and more than anything she wanted to go home.

'No. Thanks,' she added politely. Please, she silently begged. Give me an answer.

Her heart kicked against her ribs, and began thudding to a louder faster beat. Was he contemplating her offer, or merely playing a cruel game?

Did he realise how much she'd gone through in the past month, aware of her father's folly, and waiting for the axe to fall? How she'd existed on her nerves, sleeping little, haunted by what the outcome might be?

'I'll drive you home.'

She heard the words, and each one sank like a stone in a pool of negativity. 'I can get a cab to my car,' she said stiffly, painfully aware she had just enough money for the fare in her purse.

'I'll take you there.' A firm silky directive that boded ill should she dare to thwart him.

Did she utter thanks? It seemed superfluous, and she simply inclined her head as he summoned the waiter, paid the tab, then rose to his feet.

In the car she sat in silence, unable to utter a word as the vehicle slid smoothly through the streets where thinning traffic made the passage more swift.

'Where is your car?' Rafael queried as he reached the café where she worked nights.

'The next street to your left, halfway down, on the right.'

Precise directions that brought him close to the aged, barely roadworthy Mini that was her sole method of transport.

Mikayla reached for the door-clasp and turned towards him. 'I take it my offer doesn't interest you?'

He needed to take legal advice before giving a decision. Besides, it wouldn't hurt for her to wait. 'I'll be in touch within the next few days.'

It was better than a definitive *no*. 'Thank you.'

She escaped, aware that he waited until she unlocked her car, fired the engine, and then he followed her onto the main road where she turned in one direction while he took the other.

CHAPTER TWO

RAFAEL picked up the draft document delivered by courier only hours before. The pre-nup. Skilfully worded, legally scripted, it contained sufficient clauses to cover every eventuality, and then some.

He idly flicked through the pages. Fifteen months. What manner of whim had seen him extend the time-frame? Hell, he might want out in far less time. He'd even had a clause drawn up to take care of it.

There was a separate document, a waiver dropping all charges against Joshua Petersen.

Yet another document that amounted to a personal agreement between Rafael Velez-Aguilera and Mikayla Petersen.

The question was…did he implement them?

He weighed the pros and cons, and went with his gut instinct. As he had with every other decision in his life.

There was an advantage to having a mistress. The boundaries were clear-cut. Little more than a legally defined business deal.

He picked up a pen and rolled it absently between two fingers. Then he tossed it down onto the blotter and reached for a file, noted the location, checked his watch, instructed his secretary he'd be out for a while, if needed urgently he could be contacted on his mobile, then he grabbed his jacket, shrugged into it and collected his keys.

Mikayla heard the bell signalling the end of class, the end of the school day, and hid a sigh of relief. Teaching English literature to sixteen-year-old students from varied multicultural backgrounds was an art form in itself. Gaining and retaining their interest was something else again. Usually, she could make it fun.

Today she felt tired, through lack of sufficient sleep, anxiety about her father's slide in health, and acute trepidation as to whether Rafael Velez-Aguilera would make contact.

Three days had gone by since she'd shared late-night coffee with him. There had been no phone call, and the strain was beginning to tell.

'Don't forget, assignments are due in tomorrow,' she reminded as there was a swift exodus towards the door.

She tidied a stack of papers, slid them into her satchel, and slung the strap over one shoulder. Then she scooped up a small pile of textbooks, balanced them against one hip, and followed the last student out into the corridor.

Thank heaven she wasn't rostered for detention duty. It left her free to go home, set an exercise for each of tomorrow's classes, shower, eat, then call into the hospital before going on to the restaurant.

'Hi, Miss Petersen.'

She lifted her head and smiled at the student who'd paused to greet her. 'Hi, Sammy.'

'Carry your books?'

'If you like.' She handed some of them over, and dug a hand into her jacket pocket. It kind of evened up the load.

'Do ya reckon Shakespeare worked for hire?'

She spared him a wry glance. 'Perspiration, rather than inspiration?'

'Yeah.'

They reached the long stretch of paved walk leading through the grounds. Tall trees spread their leafy branches, and the afternoon sun filtered through in a dappling effect.

'Some of his plays were commissioned.' And written in a burst of creative energy, born of desperation.

'That's what I figured.'

She parked her car in the reserved bay near the entrance gates, and she headed towards it.

'You in trouble, miss?'

The query startled her. 'No. Why?'

'There's a suit by your car.'

She glanced up, and felt the blood drain to her feet. Rafael Velez-Aguilera.

'Want me to front him?'

The thought of Sammy standing up to Rafael Velez-Aguilera was laughable. Except she didn't even smile.

'It's okay.'

Sammy looked at her, then at the man who stood indolently at ease, waiting as if he had all the time in the world.

'Sure?' he queried doubtfully. He recognised the

look, respected it, and didn't know if his teacher had a clue as to the man's calibre. 'I can go get help.'

'I know him.' She didn't, really. Apart from his personal profile. Statistics, nothing that revealed the real man behind detailed facts. 'Thank you for carrying my books.' She held out her hand for them, and stifled a resigned sigh as Sammy walked right up to her Mini, waited as she unlocked the door, then transferred the books and her satchel onto the passenger seat.

'Thanks, Sammy.' It was a dismissal, and he gave her a long keen look before turning on his heel.

'You have a stalwart defender,' Rafael drawled as she pushed the door closed and stood looking at him.

Attempting to assess *why* he was here was a useless exercise. But his personal appearance had to mean something, surely?

'Yes.' The ball was in his court. She just had to wait for him to play it.

One eyebrow lifted. 'Is there somewhere we can talk?'

Her stomach clenched into a painful knot. 'There's a park not far from here.'

'Your flat would be better.'

Of course he knew where she lived. He'd have made it his business to find out. 'My landlady is against tenants entertaining in their rooms.'

He could imagine. 'Get in the car, Mikayla. I'll follow you.'

Five minutes later he drew up inside the kerb outside a double-storied brick complex that looked a little worse for wear. The fence needed repair, paint peeled off the stand of communal letterboxes, and the grass grew weeds.

'Second floor.' She opened the front door with a master key, then made for the stairs, all too aware he followed close behind.

Cooking smells permeated the papered walls, and he doubted the paintwork had seen a brush in twenty years.

Her room was just that, a room with an alcove that held a portable cook-top; beneath the counter was a bar-fridge, and there was a sink and a power-point. A door led off to what he surmised was a minuscule bathroom.

Sofa-bed, small desk with a laptop, a chair. Basic. He'd lived in much worse.

'Would you like to sit down?'

'I'll stand.'

Did he realise how he dwarfed the room? He was too tall, too broad, *too much*.

He could sense her tension, almost feel it, and had to admire her control.

'I need to set up an appointment for you with my lawyer.'

Her fingers curled into her palm. 'Is that a *yes*, Mr Velez-Aguilera?'

He didn't pretend to misunderstand. 'I have set out my terms.' His gaze was direct, inflexible. 'It is essential you fully comprehend them.'

A conditional yes, based on *his* requirements. Whatever made her think it might be different?

'The only free time I have available is between three-thirty and five.'

He withdrew his mobile, punched in a series of digits and initiated a brief conversation, then ended the call.

'Four, tomorrow afternoon.' He withdrew a card and penned a few lines on the back of it. 'The name and address.'

Mikayla inclined her head. 'Thank you. Is there anything else?'

'Not for the moment.'

'Then you must excuse me.' She walked to the door, opened it, and stood waiting for him to leave, aware of the faint amusement apparent, the slight quirk at the edge of his mouth as he inclined his head and walked past her to the stairwell.

She shut the door and leaned against it for several long seconds until the hammering of her heart settled into a steady beat.

Then she crossed to her satchel, retrieved papers and selected a textbook. Tomorrow's lessons beckoned, and with practised skill she outlined pertinent points she wanted to emphasise, then when it was done she made toast, heated a small can of baked beans, and ate the makeshift meal before heading for the shower.

Her father showed no change, and she sat with him for three-quarters of an hour before heading towards Darlinghurst.

The restaurant was busier than usual, and she stayed late in order to appease the Italian owner who seemed more than his usual temperamental self. Plates smashed, curses flew, voices rose. Even the patrons seemed more voluble and demanding than before.

It was a relief to slip out the door and walk to her car.

She was only metres away from the Mini when the hairs on the back of her neck stood on end. She turned swiftly, and saw two youths crowding her, one reaching for her bag, the other held something in his hand.

The defensive stance was automatic, the kick well-placed as it connected with a satisfying crunch. Except two against one wasn't fair odds, and she felt a stinging slash to her arm. The headlights of an oncoming car saved her from a more vicious attack, and the youths ran off, disappearing over a wall.

They'd dropped her bag in their hurry, and she picked it up, checked the catch, then moved quickly to the Mini. Once inside she locked the doors and put the car in motion.

She didn't even stop to check her arm, she just drove until she reached the flat, and it was only in the clear light she realised the amount of blood and the deepness of the gash meant it required suturing.

Who did she call at this late hour? No one, she decided grimly as she wrapped a small towel round her arm, collected her purse, and retraced her steps to the car.

There was a public hospital not too far distant. Accident and emergency would tend to it.

They did, eventually, after a two-hour wait. There

were emergencies far more urgent than hers, and there was the police statement.

It was after three when she returned to her flat, and she took the sedative the doctor advised, then pulled out the sofa-bed and crawled in beneath the covers.

Painkillers helped her get through the school day. She wore a jacket and no one suspected she had sixteen sutures in her forearm, or that it ached like hell.

Rafael Velez-Aguilera's lawyers were housed on a high floor in one of the inner city's glass-walled office towers, and she parked her car on the outskirts, then rode a bus into the city.

She made the four o'clock appointment with a minute to spare, and no sooner had she checked with reception and taken a seat than an elegantly clad woman emerged into the foyer and escorted her into a luxuriously appointed office where an immaculately attired man in his late thirties rose to greet her.

'Miss Petersen. Take a seat.' He motioned to one of four comfortable armchairs, then resumed his position behind the desk. 'Rafael has been delayed.' He pulled forward three documents, and opened the first. 'However, we can begin without him.' He handed her three copies. 'If you examine the pre-nuptial agreement, I'll go through it with you.'

He was thorough, Mikayla noted, following the document clause by clause as he clarified legalese. Every eventuality was covered.

She noted with consternation that she was to reside in Rafael Velez-Aguilera's home. Surely a mistress was a part-time lover who was maintained in an apartment of her own, and made herself available on request?

Rafael Velez-Aguilera had also changed the time-span from twelve months to fifteen, thereby lengthening her sentence.

Whatever had made her think she could stipulate terms and conditions?

He also had the right to end the relationship at any time prior to the fifteen month term. She had no such right.

Should he choose to terminate the relationship prior to the agreed upon date, the months remaining would be reduced to a percentage and calculated against the total amount owed. An amount she would be deemed liable to repay over a specified time.

Effectively, she had nowhere to move, nothing to negotiate. He held her, legally and contractually, in the palm of his hand.

Rafael Velez-Aguilera walked into the office as Mikayla cast the pre-nuptial agreement to one side and examined the second document.

She directed him the briefest of glances, her gaze cool, dispassionate.

The personal agreement was *personal*, for it covered health issues, blood tests. There was a part of her that was offended, almost insulted. Twin flags of colour heightened her cheekbones, and she was only measurably appeased to discover Rafael Velez-Aguilera had already subjected himself to similar tests.

'A necessary precaution,' the lawyer said smoothly as she stiffened at the starkly listed requirements.

The waiver followed, and she read it through carefully, ensuring the lawyer's spoken words tied in accurately with the written clauses.

'You are, of course, free to disregard these documents.'

Free to walk from this office, and have nothing to do with Rafael Velez-Aguilera. But if she took that course, she'd inherit a half-million dollar debt, which would involve her being adjudged bankrupt. Her chances of retaining her teaching position would be slim.

Whereas fifteen months wasn't a lifetime. At the end of it, she'd be free, and able to regain her own life.

The lawyer took her silence for granted.

'Do you have any questions?'

She had to strive to be businesslike. 'No.' Inside she was breaking apart.

'A doctor's appointment has been arranged following this. I have also organised a concurrent consultation with an independent legal colleague to advise you on the documentation. The test results should be through within a forty-eight hour period, a copy of which will be available to you.'

It was professional efficiency at its best. So why did she feel as if she'd just stepped onto a roller coaster?

This was what she wanted, what she'd strived for. All charges against her father dropped. She wouldn't need to wait tables every night, and she'd get to move out of her rented room.

'Thank you.' She rose to her feet and took the cards the lawyer pressed into her hand.

'The doctor's suite is on the third floor,' he informed. 'My legal colleague has a suite on the tenth floor.'

Convenient, effectively eliminating travelling time, and ensuring she could arrive at work on schedule.

Mikayla inclined her head in Rafael's direction, then walked to the door as the lawyer held it open for her, and his secretary escorted her to the bank of lifts.

The lawyer closed the door and turned towards the man who was seated comfortably to his left. 'I hope you know what you're doing.'

'You've effectively ensured everything is watertight,' Rafael drawled, waving a hand in dismissal as his long-time friend crossed to a concealed bar and withdrew a decanter of whisky and two tumblers.

Ice, a splash of whisky followed by soda, then the lawyer turned back to face the man who'd joined him so long ago in a climb to success.

'This time you're dealing with a human being, not stocks, bonds, bricks and mortar.'

'The deal intrigues me,' Rafael inclined indolently. 'As does the woman.'

'You're writing off a large sum of money.'

'One can only hope the reward for doing so will be adequate.'

The lawyer tossed back a long swallow from the tumbler. 'I wish you well.'

'*Gracias, amigo.*'

Mikayla walked into the restaurant at six, donned an apron, the stiletto-heeled pumps, and went to work.

There was no time to reflect on the afternoon's events, although lack of adequate sleep had her mixing up two orders and incurred the owner's wrath. Her arm throbbed after hours of carrying plates, trays and dishes, and she vowed if she incurred one more familiar pat on her rear, she'd walk.

Tonight she'd managed, by dint of circling the block numerous times, to find a parking space on the main street, and at eleven she collected her bag, her pay packet, and walked out onto the pavement.

'Mikayla.'

The voice startled her. The man to whom it belonged, even more.

Rafael Velez-Aguilera presented a formidable figure, his features shaded into angles and planes by the flashing multi-coloured neon sign.

'What are you doing here?'

He slanted her a hard look. 'Terminating your employment.'

Her mouth opened, then closed again. 'You can't—'

'Watch me.'

He was gone only a matter of minutes, and when he returned his expression turned her to stone.

'Get in your car. I'll follow you home.'

Her chin lifted, and her eyes blazed brilliant green fire. 'In two or three days you can tell me what to do. For now, you don't have a snowflake's chance in hell of ordering me around.'

'Brave words, *pequeña*.' His voice was deadly quiet. 'Were you as brave last night when you were attacked?'

The doctor, she surmised, who'd questioned her bandaged forearm. 'News travels fast.'

'You checked into the hospital at midnight, and out of it at three.'

My, he was thorough. 'Your sources of information are admirable.'

'Next, you'll tell me you can take care of yourself.'

'I've been doing it for a while.' She hadn't meant to sound so cynical.

'Get in the car, Mikayla.'

She did, and drove home, parked the car, then stood her ground on the pavement as his car slid into the kerb and he crossed to her side.

'I'm too tired to conduct a post-mortem.' If she didn't get inside and sit down soon, she'd fall down.

'Take a sedative. And call in sick tomorrow.'

'Yes, and no.' She began turning away from him, and offered a brief *goodnight* over one shoulder.

He let her go, aware there was little he could do to stop her.

He waited long enough to see the light in her room go on, then he slid in behind the wheel and fired the engine.

The weekend lay ahead. Monday, the test results

would be available, and he'd ensure the documentation was signed.

Even as he cleared the street and gained the main road he had to wonder why he should be concerned about a slim slip of a thing with blonde hair and green eyes.

She meant nothing to him. He had every reason to dislike and distrust her. Dammit, his legal eagle thought he was certifiably insane to consider the deal he'd drawn up for him.

So why was he not only going ahead with it, but giving way to protective instincts he would have sworn he didn't possess?

He drove home, garaged the car, then prowled the lower floor, made coffee, drank half of it and discarded the rest before entering his study, booting up the laptop, and working solidly until weariness forced him to bed.

Mikayla spent a restless night, waking several times as her arm continued to throb. At three she got up and took two more painkillers, then settled into a heavy sleep from which she didn't stir until the alarm pealed at eight.

Breakfast comprised orange juice, cereal and coffee, then she wrapped her arm in plastic and did her best to keep it dry as she showered.

Dressed in jeans and a loose cotton top, she tied a purple scarf over her hair, wound a purple scarf round the bandage, added several silver bangles, then she drove to Maisie's New Age shop at the Rocks, where her friend sold scented candles, earrings, CDs and crystals.

'Darling, great fashion accessory,' Maisie complimented. 'Totally rad.'

Mikayla merely smiled and wondered if she'd started a new trend.

Her arm still ached, but not as badly, and by Sunday it felt measurably less painful. Another day at the Rocks in the New Age shop kept her busy.

Tonight there was no need to rush home and change in order to work at the café, and she joined Maisie in a salad and carrot juice at the health food counter.

There was a strong inclination to confide, but what did she say? *Hey, Mais, I'm moving on and up. Out of the maisonette and into a mansion.* Thing was, six months ago she'd moved from a comfortable apartment into a rented room. Not exactly riches to rags, but close. For the next fifteen months, she was reversing the process.

Better she kept silent. The deal wasn't a deal until it was done, and she had yet to attach her signature to pertinent legal documents.

Her stomach executed a nervous somersault. How soon would Rafael Velez-Aguilera want to cement the relationship?

Tell it how it is, a small voice taunted. How soon will he want you to perform sexually? How often? *Every night, Mikayla.*

The thought of that large male body possessing her own stopped the breath in her throat. For the sort of money involved, he would want service. Hell, he'd want her to perform every trick in the book.

She pushed the partly eaten salad to one side, and discarded the carrot juice.

'Not hungry?'

She looked from Maisie back to the salad, and felt ill. 'No.'

She could still walk out. All she had to do was make a phone call.

'Darling, listen to me. Eat; you can't afford to lose weight.'

'So I'll have something later.' She pulled a note from her purse and placed it beneath the half-empty glass. 'I have to go.'

She drove straight to the hospital, moved through corridors, took the lift, and walked into the ward her father shared with three other patients.

And faltered as she saw Joshua Petersen had a visitor. Not a friend. None other than Rafael Velez-Aguilera.

Mikayla's expression became fierce, protective, then changed in an instant as her father turned and caught sight of her.

Rafael watched beneath slightly hooded lids as she crossed quickly to her father's side, caught each of his hands in hers and leaned forward to brush her lips against one cheek, then the other.

'You've been helping Maisie,' Joshua Petersen said in a slightly slurred voice. His smile was faintly crooked, and her heart tore at what illness had done to this once proud man. 'Look who came to visit,' he continued huskily.

She threw Rafael a glance that was intensely territorial. 'Yes, so I see.' *If you've said anything to upset him…* The warning was there, a palpable silent entity.

She was like a lioness defending a helpless cub, Rafael mused. Claws barely sheathed, and ready to spring.

'I'm sure you'd prefer to be alone,' he suggested smoothly. He inclined his head toward Joshua Petersen, then repeated the action to Mikayla as he moved to the end of the bed. 'Goodnight.'

Then he was gone, and Mikayla was left to wonder at his motive.

She stayed for an hour, grateful that her father seemed quite bright, and visiting hours were almost at an end when she slipped from the ward.

She almost expected to see Rafael's tall frame in the corridor or near the lift-well. But there was no sign of him, and she drove home, mixed two eggs together, added cheese and tomato, made toast, and ate while she checked the next day's lessons.

CHAPTER THREE

MONDAY proved to be an anticlimax. Mikayla almost expected to see Rafael waiting beside her Mini when she finished school. She drove straight to the hospital, and he wasn't a surprise visitor. That evening there was no phone call, and she spent another restless night, slept in, and was five minutes late for class.

At ten the office delivered a message for her to call Rafael Velez-Aguilera, and listed a number.

The students scrambled out the door the instant the bell rang for recess, and she collected textbooks, shoved papers into her satchel, then made her way to the pay-phone.

It was a mobile phone number, which ate coins at an alarming rate, and she must have caught him in a meeting for his tone was brief and to the point.

'Can you make it to my lawyer's office at four?'

'This afternoon?'

'Yes.'

'I can try.' Her coins ran out, and she replaced the receiver.

She took the bus into the city. It was cheaper than paying astronomical parking fees. It also made her almost fifteen minutes late.

Rafael was already there, and she entered the office, sank into a chair, and accepted a glass of chilled soda.

The lawyer regarded her thoughtfully. 'You were happy with the independent legal advice?'

Happy wasn't the right word. 'His explanation clarified all the relevant clauses.' A definition which hadn't differed from his own.

'The medical results are now available,' the lawyer continued. 'And clear.'

They couldn't be anything else, and she was tempted to offer a flip response. It wasn't the moment for facetiousness, so she merely inclined her head.

'Are you agreeable to sign the documentation?'

The trap was closing. She felt like one of King Henry the Eighth's wives about to face the guillotine.

Mikayla closed her mind to everything else except her father. 'Yes.'

It was done within minutes. Her signature first, then Rafael, and witnessed by the lawyer.

She had to get out of there. To remain and exchange meaningless pleasantries was beyond her.

'If you'll excuse me?' She rose to her feet. 'I'm due at the hospital.'

'I'll leave with you.' Rafael unfolded his length, extended his hand to the lawyer, then followed her out past reception.

'Where is your car?' Rafael queried as the lift doors closed behind them.

'At school. I caught a bus in.'

The lift slid to a halt at ground level and she emerged into the foyer.

'In that case, I'll drive you to the hospital and we can collect your car afterwards,' Rafael declared smoothly.

'There's no need for you to visit.' She needed time alone to absorb the enormity of what she'd just done.

'I'm parked across the street.'

He was so damned imperturbable, she wanted to hit him. 'No.'

They passed through the circular revolving door onto the pavement. 'The ink is barely dry, and you want to argue with me?'

There was steel beneath the silk, and she heeded the silent warning. 'I'd prefer to visit my father alone. I'd also prefer to spend tonight at my flat.' Dear heaven, *tomorrow* would come soon enough. 'I need to pack, clean, notify the landlady.' Who wouldn't be pleased at receiving twenty-four hours' notice, and who would undoubtedly demand rent in lieu.

Rafael regarded her thoughtfully for several long seconds.

She stood her ground. 'I have no intention of re-neging.'

'I would hope not,' he inclined with dangerous softness. 'Be aware I make a ruthless enemy.'

The lights changed, the 'walk' sign showed green, and together they crossed the street.

In the car she sat still, and didn't so much as offer a word during the time it took to reach the school grounds.

Mikayla barely glanced at him as she slipped out of the car. It took brief minutes to unlock the Mini and slide behind the wheel. She made to close the door, only to discover Rafael had followed her and his hand supported the door-frame.

She turned towards him with raised eyebrows. 'What now?'

'It might help if you have my residential address.'

She dived a hand into her satchel, retrieved pad and pen, then wrote down the street number and name.

'I'll expect you there tomorrow afternoon,' he drawled, and she discarded pen and pad onto the adjoining seat.

'After school finishes,' Mikayla inclined. 'When I've visited my father.'

'Six,' Rafael insisted. 'No later.'

She twisted the key and he closed the door as the engine fired, then she reversed, gained the road and joined the stream of traffic.

It was almost dark when she reached the hospital, and she stayed a while, reluctant to leave Joshua's bedside.

Visiting hours concluded, she bade her father goodnight and drove home. She'd had nothing to eat, and she fixed herself baked beans on toast, made hot sweet tea, then when she was done she picked up the phone and called the landlady.

She had expected the rent in lieu of notice, what she hadn't anticipated was the verbal abuse that came with the demand.

'Take it out of the bond security,' Mikayla instructed smoothly, knowing too well the landlady would find fault and withhold all of it.

Next, she packed everything she'd brought into the place, then she cleaned, scrubbed and tidied until her arms ached. At midnight she took a shower and fell into bed.

Mikayla woke to heavy rain. An omen? she queried silently as she quickly dressed, and she ate breakfast on the run, aware any minute the landlady would arrive to do battle.

A mild descriptive, Mikayla reflected half an hour later. Say goodbye to the bond security and furniture, the woman had it all sewn up.

It took two trips to load her belongings into the Mini, and she walked out of the flat and didn't look back.

The umbrella didn't shield her from the sleeting rain, and she got damp walking from the car park to class.

Mikayla became increasingly tense as the day progressed, and when the final bell went ending class she was as wound up as a tightly coiled spring.

At the hospital she checked with the ward's nursing station, gave details of her change of address and phone number, then went in to visit Joshua.

There was no change, and her heart bled a little for him.

All day she'd thought of a way to tell him his debt to Rafael Velez-Aguilera had been waived. He didn't need to know the truth, but he was still an astute man. She couldn't fool him into believing she'd won the lottery, or somehow managed to find such an amount of money.

In an agony of doubt, she weighed up the benefit of him knowing, or not knowing, and opted to go with a grain of honesty. Truth by omission, she acknowledged cynically.

'I have some good news,' Mikayla said gently as she pulled a chair close to his side. She took his hand in hers and soothed the slight agitated movement of his fingers against the bedcovers. 'I've reason to believe Rafael Velez-Aguilera is not going to press charges against you.'

His mouth trembled. 'Are you sure?'

'Yes.'

'But the money—'

He need never know. She'd make sure of it. 'I think it's going to be possible to work something out.'

'Is that why he visited me?'

Mikayla took hold of it like a drowning woman. 'It's most unlikely he'd have come otherwise.'

'How?'

She didn't pretend to misunderstand. 'We'll talk when I know more about it.'

A nurse came by on her rounds, and within ten minutes the dinner cart arrived.

'I'll go,' Mikayla said quietly. 'Sleep well, and I'll see you tomorrow.'

It was almost five-thirty when she edged the car out of the hospital grounds and headed towards suburban Woollahra. As she drew close she pulled over to the kerb and checked the street map, pinpointed where she needed to turn, then eased forward and picked up speed.

Her stomach twisted into a painful knot when she sighted the given street name. Old trees bordered each side, their spreading branches showing the green of seasonal spring, and she drove slowly checking numbers until she came to a wide curving driveway protected by large ornate iron gates.

They were closed. A security camera hovered on a tall pillar, and she drew the Mini to a halt, slid out and pressed the electronic button.

Almost immediately the gate mechanism began to release, and by the time she slipped back behind the wheel she was able to drive through.

Immaculate grounds, a beautiful Mediterranean double storied home, cream-plastered exterior, terra cotta and cream tiled roof, large curved windows.

It was elegant, graceful, and she slowed to a halt beneath the tiled portico less than a metre behind Rafael's Mercedes.

This was it. Her heart began to hammer in her chest as she slid from the car. She was almost at the heavy panelled double doors when one opened and Rafael stood framed in the aperture.

What did she say? Anything would sound banal, and she simply inclined her head, then turned to retrace her steps. 'My stuff's in the car.'

He was there as she reached it, and he extracted both suitcases with an ease she could only admire.

'I'll bring the rest,' she indicated. There was just her satchel, and two boxes of books.

Combined, they represented all her possessions.

'Leave the boxes,' Rafael instructed. 'I'll bring them.'

How did he think they got into the car in the first place? 'I can manage.'

'One,' he conceded. 'I'll get the other.'

'It's okay.'

She wasn't even inside the door, and already they were at odds.

'I wasn't questioning your ability,' he drawled. 'Merely cautioning against injuring your arm.'

The entrance foyer was large, tiled floor, mahogany cabinets placed in strategic positions against the walls. A wide curved ornate balustraded double staircase led to the upper floor and a magnificent crystal chandelier hung suspended from the ceiling. Wall friezes and sconces adorned the walls, together with works of art.

Wealth, Mikayla perceived, was in evidence everywhere she glanced.

'We'll take your things upstairs.'

Please, *please* tell me I have a room of my own, she begged silently as she ascended the stairs at his side. Surely privacy wasn't such a big thing to ask?

There were plenty of bedrooms, five at least, she perceived, doing a quick count of closed panelled doors.

Rafael paused in front of one, swung it open, and deposited her suitcases at the foot of the bed.

A very large bed, she saw with a sinking heart. Unless this was to be her suite, and he'd only enter it when he required her services.

'There are two walk-in robes, two en suites. I have the set to the right. You can take the left.'

Well, that cleared up any doubts she might have.

'I would prefer a suite of my own,' she informed stoically, and incurred his hard stare.

'No dice.'

'Usually a mistress maintains a separate residence,' she said quietly. 'In this instance, surely a separate suite isn't too much to ask?'

'No.' His voice was dangerously soft, lethal. 'I've already showered and changed. I suggest you do the same. We're dining out.'

'We are?' She cast a glance at her suitcases. 'I need to unpack.'

'You'll have time tomorrow.'

'No,' she said carefully. 'I won't.' Not unless she rose at the crack of dawn.

'I trust you've given notice at school?'

Mikayla stiffened. 'That wasn't mentioned in any document I signed. You work,' she stated reasonably. 'What am I supposed to do all day while you're at the office?'

Rafael saw her chin lift, and watched the green fire explode in those expressive eyes.

'Unless you expect me to also service you there?'

An interesting vision teased his mind, and he almost smiled. 'I prefer comfort. However, I'm prepared to accommodate your taste for places other than the bedroom. If that's your thing.'

Her *thing*? Dammit, she didn't have a *thing*!

'You mentioned a restaurant booking?' She crossed

to one suitcase, undid the zip fastening and retrieved an uncrushable evening pantsuit in deep emerald green and fresh underwear.

Without pausing she took out a toiletry bag and walked to the en suite on her left.

'I'll go get the remaining box and lock your car,' Rafael informed her, but she'd already closed the door.

It was a beautiful bathroom. Cool tiles, marble fittings, feminine vanity. Plenty of drawers and cupboards, a stack of luxurious piled towels.

Twenty minutes later she emerged into the bedroom and caught up her make-up bag. She'd wound her hair into a smooth twist atop her head and left two tendrils free to curl close to each temple.

She was adept at applying make-up in minimum time, and within minutes it was done.

Her own attire would pass muster. The silk jacket had long sleeves and covered her bandaged arm. It wasn't the height of fashion, but she had long acquired the habit of choosing quality rather than quantity and bought her clothes with a selective eye to style and fabric.

Rafael Velez-Aguilera looked what he was, she reflected as she re-entered the bedroom. A successful man whose sophisticated image hid a certain ruthlessness. Velvet-covered steel, she mentally attributed, as she took in the dark suit, white shirt, silk tie. There was something else, well hidden, that she couldn't quite define.

Mikayla was conscious of his swift appraisal, and

she felt goose-bumps scud the surface of her skin as she held his gaze. If he wanted to unsettle her, he succeeded, but she was damned if she'd allow him to sense her apprehension.

'Let's go,' Rafael said smoothly, and she preceded him from the room, walking at his side as they descended the staircase, then traversed the foyer to the front entrance.

She should, she supposed as the powerful car purred towards the city, offer scintillating conversation. Wasn't that part of a mistress's repertoire?

'Do I ask about your day?' Mikayla ventured, unsure whether she preferred the silence or not. Surely he could contribute *something*?

'Are you interested?'

She cast him a quick glance. 'I know what you do, of course. But I comprehend little of what it involves on a day-to-day basis.'

'Focus, concentration. Research. Always striving to be one step ahead of the competitors.'

'You're very successful.' That much was common knowledge.

'Yes.'

Most men of her acquaintance would have launched into a long spiel of their achievements, unable to resist tabling each and every one of them. Rafael Velez-Aguilera did not.

'And yours?'

'Mine?'

'Your day,' Rafael prompted smoothly.

'Where would you like me to begin? The landlady

from hell? A clash among two student factions? Conjugating verbs, discussing subjective nouns, or persuading sixteen-year-olds there is a comparison between two literary greats?'

'I'm sure it was fascinating,' he drawled as he sent the car swooping into a car park adjoining Darling Harbour.

Oh, yes, it had been that, she reflected with musing irony. She wasn't dealing with the cream of private schools. Her students came from a lower-class residential area where the parents had a seventy-five per cent divorce rate, fifty per cent unemployment; half the parents didn't know if their kids attended school or not, and the other half didn't care.

Her job was an uphill battle, and the only way she partly succeeded was to treat her students with respect and attempt to impress that education and knowledge was the weapon they needed to rise above their surroundings.

Rafael slid the car to a halt in a parking bay, and they walked through to the harbour-side and strolled the promenade. Restaurants abounded, and he led her into one where the maître d' offered a profuse welcome, then led them to a reserved table.

The food, the wine, were superb, and she chose carefully, ate with appetite and pleasure, and she declined more than one glass of excellent chardonnay.

'You come here often.' It was a statement based on the service they were given, and the fact that the staff knew Rafael's name.

'Once every week or so.'

She leaned back in her chair and surveyed him carefully. 'Not alone.'

He met her steady gaze and let a degree of humour warm his voice. 'No.'

She picked up her glass and took a small sip of wine. 'Is there any particular woman in your life who is going to be outraged by our—' she paused fractionally '—arrangement?'

His lips curved into a slight smile. 'Outraged, no.' One eyebrow arched in musing speculation. 'Surprised, yes.'

'Am I likely to be the target of her ire?'

'I am responsible to no woman. Nor do I feel obliged to offer anyone an explanation.'

Well, that certainly spelled it out.

'Would you like coffee?'

'What I'd like,' she said evenly, 'is to walk along the promenade. Perhaps cross the walkway.' And smell the fresh sea air, feel the gentle breeze on her face.

'And stop off later somewhere for coffee.'

'Yes,' she answered simply, watching as he summoned the waiter, paid the bill, then she rose to her feet and preceded him from the restaurant.

The air was cool, and there was a definite salty tang in the air. There were lights everywhere. Illuminating hundreds of windows in tall high-rise buildings, hotels, offices, apartments, reflecting on the dark harbour waters.

Music played unobtrusively in the background, and life pulsed to a changing beat. A variety of people from differing cultures provided a smattering of Italian, Greek, Japanese, Korean, and apparel varied from sophisticated evening dress to casual.

There were shops, markets to browse and, above them, a dark indigo sky with a sprinkling of stars.

Rafael watched her, saw the silky knot atop her head begin to slip, and didn't question the urge to free it.

Mikayla saw him reach out a hand, and she stood still, unable to breathe easily as his fingers removed the few pins holding the knot in place. It fell free at once, the ash-blonde weight cascading down onto her shoulders, and she tucked some of it behind each ear.

He wanted to run his fingers through the silky mass, to fist it and tug her face upwards as he took her mouth with his own.

Rafael dismissed the urge and matched his long stride to hers, prepared to indulge her for what re-mained of the evening.

They wandered for an hour, then retraced their steps and settled on a waterside café for coffee.

'Thank you,' Mikayla said quietly as they walked to the car.

'For what? A pleasant meal?'

She wasn't sure how to answer him. 'That, too.'

He disengaged the alarm and unlocked the door, then looked at her across the roof's smooth surface.

'Get in the car.'

He sounded almost grim, and she sat in silence as he eased the vehicle out of the multi-level car park, then fought city traffic as he headed towards the sub-urbs.

She made a conscious effort to regulate her breathing as they drew close to Woollahra, and by the time he brought the car to a halt inside the garage she was a mess.

Rafael cast her a thoughtful look as they reached the foyer, saw the rapidly beating pulse at the base of her throat, caught the nervous movement of her fingers on the clasp of her purse, and was intrigued.

He could sense her tension, and wondered at it. Intimacy between two consenting adults was a discovery of the senses. A mutual exploration that evoked pleasure.

A faint frown creased his forehead as they ascended the stairs. What did she think he was going to do, for God's sake? Rip off her clothes, throw her down onto the bed, and virtually rape her?

He wanted a warm and willing woman in his bed, not someone who was skittish and coy.

They reached the bedroom, and he switched on the lights, dimmed them down low, then shrugged out of his jacket and discarded his tie, watching beneath partly hooded lids as she stepped out of her heeled pumps and removed her evening jacket.

Mikayla crossed to her suitcase, extracted the knee-length cotton tee-shirt she wore to bed, and made for the en suite.

'Why bother?' Rafael drawled from across the room. 'You won't wear it for long.'

She paused, and her back stiffened, then she kept

walking and closed the door behind her. It took only minutes to change, remove her make-up and brush her teeth. The cotton tee-shirt, she decided with exasperation, outlined her firm breasts, skimmed her slender hips, and accentuated the shape of her legs.

It was better than nudity for, despite his drawled taunt, she was damned if she'd walk into the room buck naked.

Rafael, it appeared, had no such qualms, and she stood momentarily paralysed as she saw him in side profile.

His large frame was almost an art form in muscle symmetry. Tight buttocks, sculpted waist, long strongly muscled thighs. Her gaze moved upward, caught the play of muscled shoulders, the biceps, and almost died as he turned to face her.

Fine dark hair curled at his chest, narrowed down to his waist, and feathered a line to the vee couching his male appendage in an enviable state of arousal.

Dear heaven, how could she possibly accommodate him?

With no sense of exhibitionism he moved to the bed, threw back the covers, and settled onto the sheeted mattress. He leaned towards her, propped one elbow and supported his head, then he patted the empty space beside him.

She wanted to run. But there was nowhere to go. Dammit, fool that she was, she'd been the one to suggest this. Now she had to follow through.

The bed was huge. At least afterwards she could shift to one side and sleep undisturbed.

One foot after the other, she bade silently, and did just that, reaching the edge of the bed in measured steps, then she slid onto the mattress and lay still.

'Being shy is one thing, *pequeña*,' Rafael drawled. 'But you have no need to fear me.'

Want to bet? She dragged in a breath. 'We didn't meet in the most auspicious of circumstances.'

His soft chuckle almost undid her. 'So,' he began indolently. 'You would feel more comfortable if I am the one to initiate sex?'

She grabbed hold of the word and clung to it. 'Yes.'

'For a start, it would help if you came closer.'

Was he amused? She told herself she didn't care. She slid a few inches towards him, and willed the wild hammering of her heart to cease.

'A little further.'

Her hands clenched, and she slid a few more inches across the bed. 'You're enjoying this, aren't you?'

'Not particularly.'

Dear heaven. If she didn't please him, he wouldn't want her to stay. And if she didn't stay, she'd have to repay him her father's debt.

She slid further, almost within inches of that long masculine frame. She could almost feel the warmth of his body, and sense the slight musky maleness of him.

'Better,' he said quietly, and trailed gentle fingers across her cheek.

Her eyes were dark, and much too large for her face. There were circles beneath her eyes, almost

bruising the soft skin, and he knew if he had any
feelings for her, he'd let her sleep.

Instead, he leaned in close and followed the trail
of his fingers with a gentle brushing of his lips, slowly
traversing to the edge of her mouth.

He heard her breath hitch an instant before his
mouth covered hers, and he savoured the soft curve
of her lips, swept his tongue into the moist inner
sweetness, then tantalised her with an evocative tast-
ing that passed exploration and teetered close to possession.

Mikayla felt the slide of his hand on her breast, and
bit back a moan as he found one sensitive peak and
skilfully rolled it between finger and thumb.

Not content, he trailed a hand down to her waist,
then moved lower, slipping beneath the hem of her
tee-shirt as he shaped one leg, then slid to tease the
curled hair at the juncture between her thighs.

She gasped out loud as he stroked the sensitive
flesh, honed in on the highly sensitised nub, and even
as instinct scissored her legs closed, she was seconds
too late, for his fingers had slipped inside and were
creating acute sensual havoc.

'Let's get rid of this, shall we?' In one smooth
movement he lifted her and slipped the offending tee-
shirt over her head.

Was it possible for the entire body to blush? It sure
felt like it, and she saw his eyes dilate and darken as
he skimmed a hand over the smoothness of her skin.

Rafael traced every curve, each hollow, then he
lowered his head and trailed his lips over each breast,

nipped the edge of her waist, explored her navel, then travelled lower.

He couldn't, *wouldn't*...but he did. Thoroughly, with such incredible intimacy until she was on fire, caught between a myriad of sensations she daren't name.

Was she aware of the soft guttural sounds that came in gasps from her throat? The frenzied movement of her hands as she tried to lift his head free?

She was shaking, almost out of control, and he took her further, then he lifted himself over her and plunged deep inside.

And stilled. Madre de Dios.

Mikayla went from pleasure to pain in one short second as she experienced the sting of ruptured flesh, and cried out, instinctively moving further up the bed in an attempt to lessen the impact.

Rafael didn't move, and his whole body shuddered with the attempt. In damnable silence he cursed every Saint he could name, and then some.

It was several long seconds before he could talk, and when he did his voice was low and husky.

'Why in *hell* didn't you tell me?' he demanded as he cushioned his weight on his elbows. Dammit, she looked bruised, and incredibly fragile.

Her mouth shook. 'You wouldn't have believed me.'

The irony of it was that she was right. 'Why?' he reiterated, barely containing a mixture of anger and remorse.

'I never met a man I felt enough for to—wanted to

be this intimate with.' Now it was her turn to ask…
'What difference does it make?'

Sweet Mother of God. 'I could have been more
careful.' A lot more caring.

'If we're going to have a post-mortem, would you
mind moving?' If she didn't inject some black humour into the situation, she'd end up in tears.

'Oh, no, *pequeña*,' he said quietly. 'I'm not nearly
done yet.'

Her mouth shook a little. 'I am.'

'No,' he argued gently. 'You're not. Trust me.'

Trust him? How could she do that?

His lips feathered hers, seeking the softness, exploring in a way that stirred her senses.

He had the most incredibly sensual mouth, skilled
in a manner that made her forget who he was, and
why she was here with him.

She groaned out loud when he lowered his head to
her breast and took one tender peak between his teeth,
rolled it gently, then began to suckle before transfer-
ring his attention to render a similar salutation to the
other.

He felt her muscles clench around him, and he
withdrew slightly, then heard her gasp as he eased
forward a little. He repeated the movement, slowly,
and was aware when she began to pick up his rhythm.

It took a while, and it tested his control as he lifted
her legs round his waist and gently rocked back and
forth, strengthening and extending his actions until
they were in unison.

Rafael took her to the edge, held her there, then tipped her over, catching her cries with his mouth.

Afterwards he pushed the tumbled hair back from her face, and smiled a little as her eyelashes drifted down to fan out. She looked...sated, he acknowledged, and on the edge of sleep. In one easy movement he slid from the bed, filled the spa-bath with warm water, activated the jets, then returned minutes later and stepped into the scented depths with her in his arms.

Mikayla decided she was dreaming. Her conscious mind sensed the water, the slow and sensual application of soap and sponge against her skin, and refused to believe it was other than the result of her subconscious mind.

She stirred as Rafael lifted her from the bath and towelled her dry. Her protest was barely audible as he settled her in bed, then slid in and cradled her body close to his own.

CHAPTER FOUR

MIKAYLA woke with a sudden jolt, and experienced blind panic for all of two seconds before awareness dawned.

All it needed was a quick glance to determine she was alone in the large bed, and she checked the digital clock, then slid to her feet and raced to the en suite to dress, and apply minimum make-up with maximum speed.

There was time to collect her satchel, and she raced down the stairs, only to come to an abrupt halt as Rafael emerged into the foyer.

'Join me on the terrace for breakfast.'

She cast him the briefest of glances, and found she couldn't meet his gaze. 'I haven't time to eat.'

He moved forward. 'Yes, you do.'

'No, I don't.'

He offered her a wry smile. 'Do you usually argue first thing in the morning?' He removed her satchel without any effort at all and dropped it onto the tiled floor. Then he threaded his fingers through the length of her hair, tilted her head, and kissed her.

Oh, dear heaven.

Her mouth moved involuntarily beneath his, then she broke away. Only, she surmised, because he let her go. 'I'll be late.'

Dammit, she could still *feel* him inside her. Stretched, ill-used muscles contracted, and he smiled, almost as if he knew.

'It will take you only minutes to eat cereal and fruit. Coffee.'

'Are you usually this dictatorial in the morning?'

'Get used to it.'

It would appear she had quite a few things to get used to! Not least being the man himself. Even thinking about last night was enough to shred her nerves.

Capitulation seemed the wisest choice, and besides, she assured silently, she was hungry.

It would be heaven, Mikayla decided as she selected a banana and sliced it into a bowl of cereal, to sit here without the constraints of time and simply enjoy the view.

'How is your arm?'

The query was unexpected. 'Okay.' It no longer ached, but too much movement was painful. 'I go back to the hospital tomorrow to get the stitches out.'

'I'll arrange for you to see my doctor and have him do it.'

She cast him a level look. 'That's not necessary.'

Rafael leaned back in his chair and regarded her with brooding speculation. 'It will eliminate waiting for hours within the public health system.'

That much was true, but she didn't want preferential treatment. 'I imagine the hospital will want to complete their records.' She finished the cereal, discarded the coffee, and stood to her feet. 'I have to leave.' She loaded plates onto a tray and carried it through to the kitchen, a very large modern kitchen, she saw with an envious glance. Then she chose one of two doors in the hope it would lead through to the foyer.

It did, and minutes later she slid behind the wheel of her Mini and drove out through the open gates, turned right and headed towards the main arterial road leading to the inner city.

The students were restless in first class, and by the third she had distinct vibes something was going down.

Mikayla pulled Sammy to one side when the bell rang for lunch. The pretext was legitimate, she'd brought in a slim volume of some of Shakespeare's plays.

'Thanks, I'll take good care of it.'

The classroom was empty, the door shut. 'Is there something you should tell me?'

Whether or not he'd spill it was up for conjecture. 'Not if I don't want a broken leg.'

'I'm on duty during lunch-break. Is there somewhere I shouldn't be, any time from now?'

He didn't answer, and she looked at him carefully. 'Do we continue to talk in riddles, or do I give you detention?'

She glimpsed a flicker of relief, only to have it replaced by resignation.

'I have to be there.'

'You can choose not to.'

His eyes were dull, and steady. 'Yeah, sure.' Today, tomorrow, they'd get him the same. 'I gotta go.' He walked to the door, opened then closed it quietly behind him.

Mikayla had a pretty good idea of the where and how of it. The decision made, she caught up her satchel and walked the corridor to the teachers' lunch room. A quiet word, and she had an ally. Together they began a tour of duty.

Gang fighting was a common occurrence, and the school paid security officers to patrol the grounds. But the kids were smart. Far too smart for their own good, Mikayla perceived as she glimpsed a scuffle taking place close to the arts room.

The decoy. The real thing was taking place somewhere else. She had a good idea where.

It didn't help that she was right. Nor did she blench when she saw Sammy being beaten almost to a pulp. A drug deal gone wrong, or two gangs staking territory. It hardly mattered. It just needed to be stopped, for now.

Together, they did just that. The security guards added their weight, and she received a deliberately aimed elbow in her ribs for her trouble. Sammy was taken to first-aid, then sent on to hospital as he needed stitches. His mother couldn't be contacted and his father was out of town. Mikayla offered to be the chosen one, and rode with him in the ambulance.

They x-rayed him, stitched him up, and admitted him into a ward.

It was almost six when she left the ward. She found a pay-phone and rang Rafael's mobile phone.

He answered on the third ring. 'Velez-Aguilera.'

'It's Mikayla. I'm at the hospital. It'll be at least half an hour before I can get—' she couldn't for the life of her say *home* '—there.'

'Your father?'

'Sammy got beaten up. I rode the ambulance in.'

'Which hospital?'

She named it. 'I'll take a cab.'

'Wait there.' He cut the call, bit off a few pithy oaths, then went out to the car.

He pulled up in front of the main entrance fifteen minutes later. She was waiting just outside the automatic doors, her arms defensively hugging her midriff. Her hair was almost undone from its knot atop her head, and he saw the weariness, the pinched look on her expressive features as she slid into the passenger seat.

'Before I pull away from here...I trust you're not hurt in any way?'

She threw him a telling glance. 'You think I stormed in and broke it up?'

It wouldn't surprise him if she'd been instrumental in halting the bloodbath. 'From that, I deduce you weren't immediately involved?'

She could see a security officer bearing down on them. 'If you don't move, you'll get clamped.'

The Mercedes eased forward, exited the grounds, then gained speed as Rafael headed towards Woollahra.

'You didn't answer the question.'

She effected a slight shrug. 'I teach there. I was on

duty. The security guards took care of it, like they're paid to do.'

'And Sammy?'

'He has four fractured ribs, a broken arm and concussion,' she said dully. It didn't help that she'd heard one of his bones crack.

'We need to go via the school so I can pick up my car,' she reminded.

She wanted a shower, something to eat, and a good night's sleep. In that order.

It was twenty minutes before she could achieve the first, and she washed her hair, towel-dried it, then pulled on jeans and a cotton top, refrained from using any make-up, and entered the kitchen to find Rafael grilling steaks.

'Anything I can do?'

'Salad makings are in the refrigerator.'

She prepared a tossed salad, added avocado, tomatoes and celery, heated bread in the oven, then carried it to the table just as he slid steaks onto two plates.

Succulent, tender, ambrosia, Mikayla savoured each mouthful.

'You missed lunch,' Rafael noted drily as he filled both their glasses with an excellent pinot noir.

She merely inclined her head, waved away the wine, and sipped water. She took a bread roll, broke it, then ate it in between mouthfuls of steak and salad. When she was half done, she took a slow sip of wine. 'This is good.'

'*Gracias.*'

'I'll cook tomorrow night.' It was only fair.

'We're dining out.'

Her hand paused halfway between her plate and her mouth, and she cast him a steady look. 'Alone, or in company?'

'A charity ball held in the Grand Ballroom of one of the city's hotels.'

'You're throwing me in at the deep end.' For the past seven months she'd lived to work. There hadn't been time to socialise.

'We'll go shopping tomorrow.'

Mikayla lifted her fork and took time with a mouthful of food. 'I have something I can wear.'

'I'm sure you do,' Rafael responded smoothly.

'I'm meant to impress,' she deduced. 'Should I be thrilled you're prepared to spend money to see that I do?'

He sent her a look that held wry amusement. 'Are you?'

'I guess it depends.'

'On what?'

She held his gaze. 'Whether it falls under services rendered, or it's added to my existing debt.'

'Perhaps we can put a hold on labelling it?'

'For the meantime,' she conceded evenly.

He finished eating, and sank back in his chair, idly observing the neat movements of her hands as she cleaned her plate.

'Tell me why you chose teaching as a profession.' He reached forward, caught hold of his glass and savoured the wine.

'Because I thought I could make a difference,' she said simply, fascinated by his sensually moulded mouth. Remembering how it felt on her own had her reaching for her wine glass.

'And you think you can?'

She looked at him steadily. 'I hope so. I try.'

He swirled the wine, then took another swallow. 'Did you choose the school, or did the school choose you?'

'A position became available.' She effected a slight shrug. 'I was a successful applicant.'

'Among how many?'

'A few.' Not many had wanted a school with an unfavourable reputation.

'Do you enjoy teaching students with a bad attitude?'

'Is this leading somewhere, or just idle conversation?'

'Couldn't it be both?' He emptied his glass, then folded his napkin, and she watched his hands, aware how they'd caressed her skin, sought out pleasure spots and created havoc with her senses.

Her stomach did a crazy flip at the thought of what tonight would bring, and sensation arrowed deep inside, radiating throughout her body until she could no longer sit still.

'I'll clear the table and tend to the dishes.' She suited words to action, and swallowed quickly as he followed her into the kitchen.

It took only minutes to clean the grill, rinse and

stack plates and cutlery into the dishwasher, and out of habit she wiped down the servery, the sink.

'You need to acquaint yourself with the house,' Rafael indicated, leading the way into the foyer. 'Formal lounge, formal dining room, sitting room, kitchen, laundry on this side of the foyer. Opposite, a library-cum-study, a computer room, games room, and garages.'

Large rooms, beautifully furnished, a pleasing mix of marble tiles and large oriental rugs. Muted shades that were easy on the eye, the bold colours confined to prints and paintings on the walls.

'The lower floor comprises a gym, storage.'

Three levels? It was feasible, given the house was built on sloping ground, she conceded.

Mikayla discovered the upper level actually held six bedrooms, each with its own en suite, and a sitting room.

It was a large home for one person.

'I hire staff to clean and take care of the grounds.'

She opted for humour. 'Somehow it's hard to imagine you spend the weekends cleaning, mowing lawns and gardening.'

'Not in my character?'

She paused as they descended the stairs. 'Possibly.'

He arched one eyebrow, and kept walking.

'There's more to you than meets the eye,' she offered thoughtfully, and followed him down to ground level.

'A man comprised of many layers?'

Who was very careful not to reveal more than the

requisite one or two except to a chosen few, she perceived.

What did she know about him? Very little, she owned silently. His success and how he'd achieved it was common knowledge. He wore the trappings of wealth with ease. But had he always?

There was something primitive just beneath the surface. A strength that went beyond the physical. Power, he had it. But it was the hint of ruthlessness that disturbed her. A faint shiver slithered across the surface of her skin. He would make a good friend, but instinct warned he'd be a formidable adversary.

'You have an appointment at nine-thirty tomorrow to get those stitches removed,' Rafael informed her as they walked through to the sitting room.

Once there, he switched on the television and indicated an entire library of video discs. 'Choose something you'd like to watch.'

She crossed to the cabinet and examined titles. 'I can easily go to the hospital.'

'We had this argument before.'

Mikayla turned to face him. 'Well then, maybe we'll just have it again.'

'You'd opt for a minimum two hours spent in a public waiting room as opposed to a maximum five minutes in a private surgery?'

Put like that, it seemed ridiculous to oppose him. Besides, she needed to visit her father, then there was Sammy. And Rafael had mentioned shopping.

She selected a disc, then crossed to where he stood by the DVD. 'Okay.'

He took it from her, glanced at it, then inserted it into the recorder. 'That's capitulation?'

'Yes.' She sank into a comfortable single chair, slid off her sneakers, and gracefully tucked up her feet.

The previews rolled, then the film began. It was a true-life story about a gutsy young woman who'd fought society, the legal system, and won a huge settlement for a number of people adversely affected by water pollution.

It was ages since she'd been to the cinema, almost a year, if she felt like counting.

It was superbly acted; Mikayla sat entranced for more than an hour, then her eyelids began to droop and she had to force herself to remain awake.

Exhaustion, mental and physical, took their toll, and her head dipped, then slowly came to rest against the edge of the chair.

Rafael turned his attention from the screen and watched her slender form in repose. She had an air of fragility that was deceptive. Last night...

His loins tightened in memory of how it had felt to possess that slender body. The shock of discovery, absorbing her pain, and leading her beyond it to something much sweeter than he'd experienced in a long time.

He let the disc run to the end, closed the television, then crossed to the chair and lifted her into his arms. He closed lights, set the security alarm, then ascended the stairs to their bedroom.

She didn't stir, and he threw back the bedcovers, lowered her down onto the mattress, then carefully freed the zipper of her jeans and gently tugged them off. Cotton briefs came next, and he eased the top over her head, then undid her bra.

His eyes narrowed at the swelling bruise covering three of her left ribs. Surely not...? No, he'd been extremely careful. Besides, being rough with women had never formed part of his sexual repertoire.

So, it had to be today, he reflected grimly. No guesses as to how it had happened.

Rafael pulled the bedcovers over her, doused the pedestal lamp, then crossed to his side of the bed, discarded his clothes, and slid in beside her.

He picked up a book and read for a while, then sensed her move and heard the faint groan escape from her lips.

A bad dream? Or her subconscious mind forcing her to relive events of the day?

Whatever, it seemed to have a disturbing effect, and he put the book aside, turned off the light, and drew her close.

In sleep, she rested against him, welcoming his warmth and the comfort he offered.

Moonlight filtered in through the partly closed shutters, casting shadows across the room.

Rafael lifted a hand and smoothed a few strands of hair from her face, then he leaned forward and brushed his lips to her temple.

Mikayla stirred just before dawn, and became aware she wasn't alone. For a few brief seconds she lay perfectly still, then she moved, changing position slightly.

She turned her head slowly, and saw Rafael's features in repose. Relaxed in sleep, he lost some of the hardness, and she looked her fill, noting the dark eyelashes with a slight upward curl at their tips. Olive, textured skin showed a dark shadow at the edge of his cheekbones that ran down past the edge of his jaw.

She had the strangest desire to reach out and trail her finger-pads over his cheek, feel the slight roughness, then trace the curve of his mouth.

What would he do if she gave in to temptation?

There was a part of her that wanted to have his mouth cover her own. To experience the *tendresse* he'd shown her after his initial possession. The slide of his hands on her skin as they conducted a provocative discovery of each pleasure pulse.

'*Buenos dias.*'

Her eyelashes opened wide at the sound of that husky greeting.

'I thought you were asleep.'

Did he tell her that he slept like a cat, aware of the slightest sound, the faintest movement? Even now, years down the track, it was an ingrained habit he couldn't break.

He'd been conscious of her watching him for the past five minutes.

'You rested well.'

How could he know that? 'I fell asleep watching

the film.' Which meant he must have carried her to bed *and* undressed her. 'I guess it's a bit late to be—'

'Embarrassed,' he completed, interpreting her fleeting expression, and his mouth curved into a musing smile. 'A little.'

'I should get up.'

'No,' Rafael refuted gently. 'You shouldn't.'

He watched those emerald depths dilate and become dark, and her lips shook a little as he raised a hand and brushed some of her hair back behind one ear.

He leaned forward and sought the soft hollow of her throat, savouring it with his mouth, then he softly bit the skin and felt her body contract in response.

The curve of her neck tasted sweet, and he nuzzled there, grazing it with his teeth before trailing a path to the edge of her shoulder.

One hand splayed over her hip, then slid up to her breast, and created an erotic pattern with each sensitive peak.

His head lowered, and she arched her neck as he sought her breast and savoured the soft skin, then gently suckled until liquid fire surged through her body, dispensing inhibitions as she reached for him, wanting, needing closer contact.

With a tentative hand she sought his chest and threaded her fingers through the whorls of dark hair, tugging a little, before slipping to his waist, pausing momentarily, then sliding over his hip.

She wanted to feel the power that had both shocked and pleasured her.

He sensed her hesitation, covered her hand with his own, shifted it several inches, and caught her indrawn breath.

Her touch was as light as a butterfly's wing, and he swallowed a faint groan at her hesitant exploration. Man at his most vulnerable, he reflected silently.

The covers hit the floor as he swept them off the bed, and her body shook as he slid her leg over his hip and pulled her in close. One hand shaped her buttock, then conducted an intimate exploration that drove her almost wild with its intensity.

She clung as he slowly slid into her, and she couldn't prevent an involuntary gasp as sensation spiralled deep inside, building with each movement he made until she became caught up with a primitive rhythm, consuming, all-encompassing, so that she was so much a part of it there was nothing else. Only the man, the moment, and elemental passion.

It seemed an age before Mikayla drifted slowly down in a helpless state of exquisite inertia.

Rafael trailed his fingers over her hip, slid down her thigh to her knee, lightly kneaded her calf muscles, then traced a path up her inner thigh to where they lay joined.

She was intensely sensitive, and the merest touch was enough to stir the hunger into primitive life.

Dear heaven, what was he trying to do?

It was bewitching sensuality at its most mesmeric as treacherous desire tore the breath from her body, and she climbed higher than she thought it possible to reach and still survive.

She marvelled at his level of control. His breathing hadn't quickened, and she was willing to swear his heart wasn't hammering in his chest as hers did.

How could he appear so unaffected, when she was a quivering mess?

If she cared about him, she might have smiled and teased him a little, brushed light kisses over that broad muscular chest, perhaps even tantalised each dark male nipple with the edge of her teeth until he growled for mercy and hauled her up to possess her mouth with his own.

She might also take delicious liberties with his male body, just to hear the breath hiss between his teeth, to feel the surge of male power as he took control.

Instead, this sharing of sexual intimacy was too new, too fragile, for her to feel in any way emboldened, and she lay quietly, aware of the drift of his fingers, the light kisses he pressed to the curve of her shoulder.

She must have slipped into a light doze, for when she woke she was alone, and she heard the shower running, checked the digital clock, then collected a change of clothes and made for the en suite.

CHAPTER FIVE

RAFAEL insisted he accompany her into the doctor's surgery. Worse, he stayed while her arm was examined and the stitches removed. Next he committed the unforgivable and mentioned the bruise discolouring her ribs.

Mikayla threw him a look that spoke volumes, and became further enraged at his musing appraisal as the doctor probed the swelling and pronounced no bone damage.

'You are,' she declared in a voice seething with angry frustration the instant the lift transported them down to ground level, 'impossibly dictatorial.'

He lifted one eyebrow. 'Are you done?'

'No, I'm not *done*.'

The lift slid to a halt, and they exited the building, walked to where the car was parked, and she sat in silence as he drove to Double Bay.

The boutiques sold expensive designer gear, much of it original, and the price tags, she knew, were astronomical.

Mikayla slid from the car and stood on the pavement as he crossed round to her side. 'I don't think—'

'I'm not asking you to think,' Rafael drawled, and held her gaze when she glared at him.

'You want to flash plastic in some of the most expensive places in town? *Fine*.'

Mikayla had to concede he had excellent taste. Within two hours she'd acquired two long evening gowns, two cocktail dresses, shoes, and an exquisite two-piece evening suit.

'Lunch,' Rafael announced as he placed the various emblazoned carry-bags into the boot of the car and locked it.

He chose the Ritz-Carlton, selected à la carte, and regarded her with a tinge of amusement as she ordered soup followed by a smoked salmon starter.

'No main meal?'

She offered him a solemn look. 'I'd have been happy with a sandwich and coffee.'

'You are not impressed?'

Mikayla held his gaze. 'Am I meant to be?'

'It wasn't my intention.'

They were, nonetheless, gaining some attention from a few fellow diners. 'You wanted to be seen?' she hazarded, and saw his eyes darken fractionally.

'Not particularly.'

She'd chosen to wear a slim-line skirt and blouse, and had added a stylish jacket. It wasn't designer gear, but it was suitably fashionable.

'In that case… Thank you.'

'For what?'

'The clothes,' she said simply. 'The meal.'

Was it an act? Somehow he didn't think so. 'I shall see that you do…' He paused, then said deliberately, 'Thank me.'

Don't confuse acquisitions as anything other than a pleasant bonus, she chided silently. It just forms part of the packaging and presentation. After all, a mistress must be well dressed.

The soup was delicious, the salmon divine, and she declined wine and settled for an innocuous fruit spritzer.

'I'd like to go visit my father,' Mikayla ventured as they sipped black coffee. 'I didn't get to see him yesterday. And then, there's Sammy.'

'Each at different hospitals,' Rafael indicated, and she looked at him carefully.

'I'll ensure I'm back at the house in time, if you'll tell me when we need to leave.'

'Just after six.'

She spared a glance at her watch and saw it was well after two. 'I visit Joshua every day. And Sammy has no one.' Not anyone who cared, she added silently.

He summoned the waiter, paid the bill, then rose to his feet.

'I'll expect you home at four thirty. No later,' he warned as they reached the car.

Parking anywhere near either hospital was the pits and, being the weekend, visitors were many. However, her father's anxiety fled the minute she walked up to his bed, and she spent half an hour with him before driving several miles to visit Sammy, who was looking a bit worse for wear as the bruising showed more vividly.

'You came.'

She'd brought a slim volume of Dickens, and bottled fruit juice. 'I can't stay long.'

'It's okay.'

She stopped at the nurses' station on the way out, queried his progress, checked on the expected length of his stay, then walked almost half a mile to reach her car.

It was a few minutes past four thirty when she raced upstairs, and the instant she reached the bedroom she began discarding clothes, shoes.

Unpacking had been achieved after breakfast that morning, and she caught up fresh underwear and entered the en suite to shower, wash her hair, then she wound a towel sarong-wise round her slim curves and began the process of applying make-up, styling her hair before emerging into the bedroom to dress.

The gown was stunning in shimmering peacock green and blue, slim-fitting, a low scooped neckline, with a single shoestring strap over each shoulder. There was a matching wrap, which cleverly positioned, hid the healing wound on her arm.

Her only jewellery was a slender gold chain with a small diamond pendant and matching earrings gifted by her parents for her twenty-first birthday.

She'd chosen to sweep her hair high in an elegant knot atop her head, and she slid her feet into the delicately balanced heeled evening shoes as Rafael entered the bedroom.

He was freshly shaven, his hair gleaming from a recent shower, and he looked the epitome of sophis-

tication in superbly tailored black trousers and a crisp
white shirt.

Mikayla endeavoured to steady the increasing beat
of her heart at his breadth of shoulder, the vee of olive
skin at his throat exposed by a few shirt buttons that
remained to be fastened.

He was an imposing man. In every way, she added
silently. He had the grace of a jungle cat, fluid body
movement that owed much to superb physical fitness.

Within minutes he fastened cuff-links, buttoned his
shirt, added a bow-tie, then he snagged his jacket and
shrugged into it.

'Tell me something about the evening,' Mikayla
asked as the car neared the city. It was cool, and the
roads were slick from a recent shower of rain. 'The
charity.'

'The Leukaemia Foundation,' Rafael informed her,
sparing her a quick glance.

'A worthy cause.'

'One of a few I choose to support.'

They reached the hotel, and he drew the Mercedes
to a halt outside the main entrance, requested valet
parking, and Mikayla slid from the passenger seat.

They took the lift to another floor, and entered the
extensive foyer adjacent the magnificent ballroom.
Waiters and waitresses worked the room offering
wine and champagne while the city's social elite
sipped, gossiped, and kept an eagle eye on arriving
fellow guests.

'Darling. There you are.'

Mikayla turned slightly to see a tall dark-haired

young woman almost upon them. Everything about her was perfection, from the top of her exquisitely coiffed head to the toes of her European imported shoes.

Oh, my. Those beautifully lacquered nails, the gown...the jewellery.

Was it her imagination, or did she sense Rafael's wariness?

'Sasha,' he greeted smoothly.

'Aren't you going to introduce us?'

'Of course. Sasha Despojoa. Mikayla Petersen.'

The five-second once-over, Mikayla acknowledged, aware she had been assessed and dismissed.

'I don't believe we've met,' Sasha purred. 'Are you new in town?'

New to this part of town, she felt inclined to offer, and merely smiled. 'No,' she said simply.

Sasha arched one delicate eyebrow. 'I assume you know each other quite well?'

Twenty questions? If Sasha wanted to play, Mikayla felt able to match her. 'Rafael is—' She paused and cast him a deliberately musing smile. 'A special friend.'

Sasha's intrigue was evident. 'I see.'

No, you don't, Mikayla silently denied.

'We'll talk.'

Really? It didn't need three guesses to pin down the subject. Sasha seemed bent on eating Rafael alive. The smile, the touch of her impeccably lacquered nails on his sleeve. The way she moistened her lips.

Blatant invitation attractively wrapped in sizzling sensuality.

'I believe we're seated at the same table,' Sasha enlightened, and Mikayla lowered her lashes fractionally.

This *was* going to be a fun evening.

'You'll excuse us?' Rafael interceded indolently. 'There are some friends I'd like Mikayla to meet.'

'The stunning Sasha is one of your used-to-be's?' She queried, *sotto voce*. 'Recent, I'd say.'

He cast her a lazy glance. 'Yes.'

'Do I need to watch my back?'

'I didn't promise her a—'

'Rose garden?' Mikayla intruded cynically.

He smiled at her quaint turn of phrase. 'No.'

'Ah,' she chastised mildly. 'But I'm willing to bet she has been mentally redecorating the house and changing the furnishings.'

'I rarely invite a woman to stay overnight in my home.'

Now why did she feel relieved the bed *she* shared with him hadn't been shared with others?

'Prefer the hotel, motel, her place, huh?'

'None of your—'

'Business,' she concluded with a sweet smile. 'I know.'

He wanted to reach out, cover her sassy mouth with his own, and change the mischievous sparkle in those deep green eyes to drenching sensuality.

'Don't push your luck,' he drawled, and caught her winsome smile.

'I wouldn't dream of it.'

Together, they mixed and mingled until the grand ballroom doors opened and uniformed staff began directing guests to their tables.

The starter was served within minutes of everyone being seated, and Mikayla forked the prawn cocktail with enjoyment.

Rafael ordered an excellent chardonnay, and she took a few cautious sips while the Foundation spokesperson gave an introductory speech.

There were ten people to each circular table, and it amused her to see Sasha had deliberately seated herself directly opposite Rafael.

Now there was a woman who should have taken up acting as a profession, Mikayla perceived, watching the carefully choreographed movements, the subtle and occasionally not so subtle gestures as Sasha employed coquetry in an attempt to attract Rafael's attention. And any other man who happened to be within visual distance.

Models took to the catwalk and showed a variety of haute couture whilst the main course, comprising breast of chicken in a delicate sauce accompanied by artistically displayed vegetables, was served.

There was a comedian, a singer, and a five-minute video displayed on the huge visual screen on-stage showing poignant scenes of young children stricken with the disease.

It was emotionally moving, and a vivid reminder for patrons to dig deep into their pockets to support the charity.

The evening was well organised, the pace professional, and there wasn't much opportunity for discussion until the lights went up and the waiters began serving dessert and coffee.

Guests began moving between tables, catching up with friends, and it didn't take long for Sasha to slip into a temporarily vacated seat close by minutes after Rafael's attention was caught by a colleague.

'Have you known Rafael for very long?'

A continuation of the inquisition, Mikayla decided wryly. 'No,' she said with studied politeness.

'Not very forthcoming, are you, darling?'

'How forthcoming do you want me to be?' she countered.

'You must forgive me for appearing curious. Rafael and I have been good—' she paused delicately '—friends, for a while.'

'Really?' Mikayla offered sweetly.

Sasha waited a beat. 'Intimate friends,' she revealed with deliberate emphasis.

'So... Hands off?'

'I knew you'd understand.'

'Shouldn't you be having this conversation with Rafael?'

'I don't think so. He's merely teasing me by escorting you here tonight.'

Mikayla tried to feel sympathy for her, and failed. 'If you'll excuse me for a few minutes?' She stood to her feet and caught hold of her evening purse, intent on escaping to the nearest powder room.

Rafael saw her leave the table, glimpsed Sasha's

satisfied smile, and was sure he could guess the conversation almost word-for-word. Sasha, he knew, was adept at aiming a sharp verbal arrow. On the other hand, he held little doubt Mikayla could hold her own.

It was interesting how women felt the need to repair their make-up, he mused, when most men were turned on by a natural look.

Something which brought a vivid recollection of the petite slender blonde-haired witch who'd woken in his arms in the early morning hours and conducted a tentative exploration that had driven him almost to the brink.

She was a willing pupil, whose pleasure brought a familiar tightening to his loins. There was nothing contrived in her response, just a mixture of shocked surprise followed by intense delight as he led her on a sensual path to sexual discovery.

Rafael brought his conversation to an end as Mikayla re-entered the ballroom, and he watched her passage as she moved towards him. Aware, also, that he wasn't the only one observing her approach.

Staff were speedily dismantling the catwalk, and clearing space for a dance-floor while a DJ set up equipment to one side of the stage.

Mikayla reached Rafael's side, then slid into her seat, and she declined a second coffee in favour of iced water.

'Some more wine?'

She met his gaze and held it. 'No, thanks.'

The DJ spun his first disc, and a few couples took to the floor.

'Dance with me, Rafael.'

She recognised the voice, wondered at Sasha's audacity, and offered Rafael a musing smile. 'Have fun.'

For an instant she glimpsed dark amusement before it was quickly masked and replaced by polite charm, and she watched as Rafael led the dazzling Sasha onto the dance floor.

They looked good together, she conceded. Almost too good. For there was an easy familiarity existent that brought a pang of something she immediately discounted as jealousy, or envy.

'I hate to see a beautiful young woman sitting alone.'

Mikayla turned at the sound of that smoothly spoken voice, and offered a polite smile as an attractive young man slid into an empty seat.

'Can I get you some wine? More coffee?'

Interesting, she mused. It was a while since someone had attempted to chat her up in a social situation. Perhaps she should just kick back and enjoy the experience.

'No, thanks.'

'Are you with anyone?'

Now there was a question! One perhaps she could avoid for a few minutes. 'I didn't catch your name.'

'Forgive me,' he said quickly. 'Anthony Moore-Jones. And you are?'

'Not yours, my friend,' Rafael drawled with a dangerous silkiness that sent ice slithering down Mikayla's spine.

Anthony's reaction was one of surprised dismay, and he quickly rose to his feet. 'I'm sorry. I had no idea.'

'Now you do,' Rafael said with deceptive mildness.

'Yes. Yes, of course.' His eagerness to be gone was almost comical. 'If you'll excuse me?'

'Do you normally eat young men for supper?' Mikayla queried lightly as he occupied the seat Anthony had so rapidly exited.

'Only those who infringe on my territory.'

'Nice to know my place.'

'Don't be facetious,' he chided, aware of Sasha's curiosity.

'Perhaps you should enlighten those interested just what Mikayla's place is?'

Mikayla looked at Rafael and arched an enquiring eyebrow as he leaned back in his seat.

'Mikayla lives with me.'

Sasha's gaze hardened slightly. 'As your guest?'

He made no attempt to soften the blow. 'My mistress.'

There was a faint gasp, a brief glimpse of inimitable fury, before it was quickly masked. 'Really, darling?' She recovered well. 'You could have told me.'

'We were occasional lovers,' Rafael said steadily. 'When the mood, the moment, suited both of us. It was never permanent.'

'Your mistake,' Sasha declared coolly as she col-

lected her evening purse and disappeared through the
crowded ballroom.

'That was cruel.'

Rafael's eyes held an expression she didn't care to
define. 'It was the only truth she could understand.'

Mikayla looked at him, saw the strength, the
power, and the ruthlessness. 'I don't think I like you.'

His lips curved into a twisted smile. 'You are not
required to *like* me.'

'No,' she said steadily. 'Just satisfy you for the
duration of my sentence.'

'Careful, *pequeña*,' he warned softly, intrigued by
the way the colour of her eyes deepened to the darkest
emerald.

'I'm not afraid of you.'

'Brave words.'

'If I could,' she began quietly, 'I'd walk out of here
and get a cab.' Her chin lifted a fraction. 'But I have
no money, and I'm stuck with you.'

His musing smile made her want to *hit* him, and
she watched in disbelief as he stood, caught hold of
her hand and drew her to her feet.

'Dance with me.'

'You have to be joking!'

She had little choice but to follow...unless she
caused a scene by openly opposing him.

The music changed pace from heavy metal to bal-
lad as they reached the dance floor, and he turned her
into his arms. He held her close, and she felt his lips
brush her hair, then slide to her temple.

The anger began to fade, although she tried hard to

maintain it. Instead she fought against an intrusive warmth that seeped stealthily through her veins, heating her blood, invading sensitive pleasure pulses until it touched her sensual heart.

It would be easy to sink in against him, to have her body move as one with his. To feel the tell-tale quiver as his lips sought the vulnerable curve at the edge of her neck.

Instead, she forced herself to remain stiff and unresponsive, and she was willing to swear she heard his faint husky chuckle.

The temptation to deliberately stand on his toes was great, and she suffered…as he knew she suffered, and it was that which riled her even more.

It was well after midnight when Rafael brought the car to a halt inside the garage, and Mikayla didn't have the pleasure of stalking into the house ahead of him, for the simple reason she possessed no key, had no access to security codes.

As soon as they reached the entrance foyer she made straight for the stairs, aware that his ascent was more leisurely.

She entered the bedroom several seconds ahead of him, and she slid off her shoes, removed her pendant and earrings, then reached for the zip fastening on her gown.

Beneath it she wore a full-length slip and briefs, no bra, and she caught up a tee-shirt and pulled it over her head, then carefully hung up the gown.

Without a word she moved towards the bedroom door.

'Don't even think about sleeping in another room.'

Mikayla turned back to look at him, and almost died at the darkness evident in his gaze. His jacket and tie lay discarded, he'd unbuttoned his shirt, removed his cuff-links, and was in the process of stepping out of his trousers.

'I don't want to occupy the same bed with you tonight.'

'Do you know how easy it will be for me to have you want to?'

She opened the door, walked into the gallery, and closed the door quietly behind her.

Would he follow her? She told herself she didn't care, any more than she cared less that she couldn't win against him. It was the principle, she assured silently as she opened another door and crossed to the window.

It was a dark moonless night, and all she could see of the grounds were shadows. In the distance pinpricks of light outlined suburban streets, and there was the occasional gaudy flash of neon, red, green, blue, illuminating an advertisement.

She sensed rather than heard him walk into the room, and knew that he came to stand behind her. Hell, she hadn't even made it difficult for him to locate her.

He didn't say a word. Instead he stepped in front of her and covered her mouth with his own. There was no cajoling, just the sweep of his tongue, and the slow sweet heat of sensual skill as he evoked a response she was reluctant to give.

No part of his body touched hers, except his mouth, and he sensed the moment she gave in, sighing her capitulation as her hands crept up to his neck, then linked together at his nape.

Rafael cupped her face, and deepened the kiss, then he smoothed a hand over her shoulder, skimmed her waist, then rested momentarily on her hip before slipping beneath the hem of her tee-shirt and curving over her bottom, urging her close as his fingers slipped inside her.

Did it matter that she gave in to the magic of his touch? Or that if he won, she lost? Because if this was losing, she reflected, it was no loss at all.

He took her high, breathing in her soft cries as she reached the heights, and he held her there, then tipped her over and caught her as she began to fall, only to lift her high and wrap her legs around his waist.

She was heat and passion, and he plunged deep inside, withdrew, and repeated the action again and again until he felt her shuddering release.

Mikayla buried her face against his neck as he walked back into the bedroom, then followed her down onto the bed.

Seconds later she gasped as he rolled over onto his back, and held her as she straddled his hips.

His eyes were dark, his hand gentle as he brushed the tips of his fingers over her breast, circled it, then teased the tender peak before trailing down to the triangle of hair at the apex of her thighs.

He sought the tight bud of her clitoris, and saw her eyes flare as he stroked until she went wild, then he took her up and over, held her there, then his hands cupped her face as he brought her mouth down to his in a kiss that robbed the breath from her throat.

Mikayla doubted she could stand any more, but he proved she could as he gave her the power to take the ride of her life.

Afterwards she sank down against him, too enervated to move, and she felt the soft slide of his hand as he skimmed the length of her spine.

He settled her head into the curve of his shoulder and soothed her tousled hair, and it was there she drifted to sleep, unaware of the covers being drawn, or the light brush of his lips as he carefully disengaged her and curled her against his side.

Mikayla stirred through the night, haunted by a dream where she was being chased down a dark alley, and no matter how fast or how far she ran he was there right behind her.

Hands caught and held her, and she cried out as she fought to be free of them. She heard a husky voice curse, then light blinded her, and she saw that it was Rafael who held her, and the alley melted away as she recognised the bedroom, the house.

Rafael felt the shaking begin to subside, and held her close. 'Sweet Mother of God, what or who were you running from?'

When she didn't answer, he lifted her face, glimpsed the tear-drenched eyes, and swore softly. 'Mikayla?'

'I don't know. I didn't see his face.'

The youths who attacked her, witnessing Sammy's gang fight... Or Rafael Velez-Aguilera? Dear God, the latter didn't sit well.

The subconscious mind could wreak havoc, he knew. There were occasions when he woke in a sweat after nightmares transported him back to his youth when times had been tough and often cruel. Years that had shaped and hardened him into the man he was today.

'You're with me,' Rafael reassured gently, soothing her. 'Nothing can hurt you here.'

For now, Mikayla conceded shakily, as she deliberately turned her mind to her father and happier times.

CHAPTER SIX

MIKAYLA woke late, rolled over in bed and glimpsed the time, then raced for the shower.

Rafael joined her there, stilled her hurried movements, and met her anguished frown.

'What's the rush?'

'I forgot to phone Maisie. I'm meant to help out in her shop at the Rocks. Oh, dammit!' She cursed as the soap slipped to the tiled floor, and she bent to pick it up.

'Stand still,' he commanded, taking the soap from her nerveless fingers. 'And explain.'

'Maisie is a friend. I work for her at the weekends. I told her I couldn't help out yesterday, but I forgot about today. It'll be busy,' she said wretchedly. 'And she'll be expecting me.' She became aware of his actions with the soap, and tried to push his hand away. 'Will you stop that?'

His mouth curved with sensual warmth. 'No.'

'Rafael—' she faltered as her body began to respond of its own accord.

He handed her the soap. 'You can return the favour.'

Something which had dangerous implications. 'I don't think so.'

'Your arm is healing well.'

There was just a thin red line, and the suture marks were already beginning to fade.

She looked at him, saw the slumbering passion, and knew if she stayed it would be for a while. 'I really have to go.'

He leaned forward and kissed her, thoroughly. 'Then go, *pequeña*.'

'I'll be there until late afternoon.'

'After which you'll visit your father. I'll cook dinner.' He saw her hesitate, then he said quietly, 'Ten seconds, Mikayla, or you won't get out of the house for at least an hour.'

She escaped, and minutes later she dressed in jeans, a loose top, pulled on sneakers, then caught her hair together, grabbed her purse, her keys, and raced downstairs.

It proved to be a hectic day, and neither she nor Maisie had a minute to spare until late afternoon when trade began to lessen. Only then was there time to tell Maisie of her move, and her probable inability to help out in future.

'*Woollahra?* You're kidding me, right?' Maisie's eyes narrowed. 'And you're living with him and having sex?' She whistled through her teeth. 'Man, he must be something. You always vowed you wouldn't do it without a ring.'

Mikayla managed a light shrug. 'A girl can change her mind.'

'Not you, sweetie. You always had such strong principles.'

She wanted to say she'd had no choice but to bend

them. Except the less Maisie knew of the truth, the better.

'Why don't you finish up early and go on to the hospital? It's quietened down, and I can manage.'

'Are you sure?'

'Go, Mikayla. Give me a call sometime, huh? Don't lose touch.'

'I won't.'

Joshua seemed very tired when she visited, and her heart dropped a little. The head nurse was non-committal, merely offering that a gradual slide in his well-being was inevitable.

Mikayla stayed for a while, and helped feed him. A slow process which dismayed her, for he showed little interest in food.

Rafael took one look at her pale features as she entered the kitchen, and made an instant decision to delay dinner.

'What is it?' He turned down the heat on the stove-top, and crossed to her side. 'Your father?'

She relayed the nurse's update, aware Rafael knew the outcome as well as she did.

He lifted a hand, caught hold of her chin and tilted it. There were shadows beneath her eyes, and she was pale. 'Did you manage lunch?'

She could hardly remember. 'We were busy. A sandwich, I think.'

He felt a surge of angry frustration, briefly wondered at it, then banked it down. 'I've made pasta with a seafood sauce.' He took down another glass, poured in some wine, and handed it to her.

'It'll put me to sleep,' she protested.

Maybe that wasn't such a bad thing. 'Drink.' He touched the rim of her glass to his own, then took a measured swallow, watching as she sipped a little from the glass.

'I should shower and change.'

'Why don't you go do that, while I finish up here?'

She placed the glass down onto the servery, then went upstairs. It was ten minutes before she re-emerged feeling measurably refreshed. She'd donned tailored trousers and a buttoned blouse, left her hair loose, and touched colour to her lips.

Rafael was in the process of apportioning servings onto two plates when she entered the kitchen, and the tantalising aroma of hot garlic bread teased her taste-buds as she collected her glass and crossed to the table.

'Mmm, this is good,' she complimented after the first mouthful.

'Gracias.' He selected a piece of garlic bread, tore off a piece, and ate it.

Mikayla witnessed the fluid movement of his hands, their strength, their tactile skill, and found her-self expressing a need to know more about him.

'Have you lived all your life in Australia?'

'Idle curiosity about my roots?' he queried lightly as she met his gaze.

'Interest,' she corrected.

'The youngest of three children whose parents em-igrated to New York from Barcelona and failed to discover the American dream.' There was no point in revealing the screaming poverty that followed. 'My father managed to tie up a job in Sydney, worked hard, and the family followed a few years later.' *Life* had taught him more than he ever wanted to know.

Mikayla regarded him steadily, aware there were blanks and wondered at them. 'You finished school here, and went on to university.'

'Yes.' Rafael finished the food on his plate, and pushed it to one side. 'And you?'

'Middle-class upbringing, private schooling, sports, university, friends, the usual social existence.' She gave a light shrug. 'Nothing of any particular note.'

'Until your mother suffered an accident that left her in a coma and on life support.'

The loss had been traumatic. Worse was the discovery of her father's embezzlement, his own failing health. The combined knowledge had led her to offer herself in a desperate deal with the man who now sat opposite.

'It hasn't been a good year.' An understatement, if ever there was one.

'And now you are beholden to me.' He glimpsed the way her eyes dilated, and saw the tilt of her chin. Pride, and courage.

'Yes.' Fourteen months, three weeks and four days. More than four hundred nights with a man who was beginning to get beneath her skin. Someone she wanted to hate. Instead, her body sang beneath his skilled touch, and her senses soared in a way she'd never in her wildest imagination deemed possible.

She had to put some space between them, and she

stood to her feet, collected plates and utensils and carried them to the sink.

Rafael watched her, saw the squared shoulders, the carefully controlled movements as she rinsed and stacked, and he resisted the urge to go to her, pull her into his arms and cover her mouth with his own.

They had the night, and he intended to make use of it in a way that offered him more pleasure than he'd been gifted in a while.

'You mentioned sports. Any one in particular?'

He saw her pause, but she refrained from looking at him.

'Tennis, swimming.' She dealt with a pot, scouring it with a thoroughness that didn't escape him. 'Tae-bo.'

'There is a tennis court, a pool, and a well-equipped gym on the premises,' he drawled. 'Choose one.'

Now she did glance in his direction, and he glimpsed surprise, faint interest.

'Tennis.'

Rafael inclined his head. 'Half an hour?'

'Okay.'

She was there, waiting for him, and they warmed up with a few volleys before playing in earnest.

He won, of course. She expected no less, for he had the height, the breadth of shoulder, the killing power to trounce her off the court. Except he didn't, nor did she get the feeling he was deliberately down-sizing his game for her benefit

'Enough,' Rafael called. 'Or you'll damage your arm.'

Together they entered the house, and ascended the stairs.

'Care to join me in the spa?'

Mikayla cast him a quick glance, then shook her head. 'I'll take the shower.'

She had yet to lose her inhibitions, he mused thoughtfully, anticipating the day when she initiated and exulted in sexual pleasure. He wanted the teasing delight of her touch, her soft husky laughter as she drove him to the brink, then held him when he shuddered helplessly in her arms.

Was she aware how much power she held in her hands? Somehow he doubted it.

'Pity,' Rafael drawled with musing mockery as he entered the bedroom and made straight for his en suite.

She collected a change of clothes and headed for the shower, indulging in leisurely ablutions before emerging to dress in jeans and a rib-knit top. An adept twist of her wrist saw her hair pinned up, and she negated the use of make-up.

Mikayla entered the bedroom and came to a sudden halt at the sight of Rafael, sans clothing of any kind. He hadn't even had the decency to hitch a towel at his hips.

He looked up, caught her expression, and lifted an eyebrow. 'My state of undress offends you?' He crossed to a chest of drawers, extracted silk briefs and stepped into them.

But not before she caught sight of a small oriental symbol tattooed on the upper curve of one buttock.

'It represents honour above all things,' he interpreted quietly.

She met his gaze and held it. 'Should I question why?'

He didn't say anything for several seconds. 'I considered it appropriate at the time.'

'And chose not to have it removed.'

A vivid reminder of another time, another life. 'No.'

He extracted black jeans, pulled them on, then he took a black knit polo shirt and tugged it over his head.

The dark clothes lent him a dangerously ruthless look, and just for an instant she had a glimpse of what he might have been. What he could become, if driven too far.

'I have some papers to mark,' Mikayla said quietly. 'Tomorrow's lessons to set. It'll take me a few hours.'

He could well use the time in the computer room. 'I'll make coffee.'

Mikayla liked the friendly feel of the kitchen, and she spread everything out on the table, weighing the Education Board curriculum with the week's classes.

It was eleven when she slid papers and textbooks into her satchel, and she stretched her arms high above her head to ease stiff muscles. Minutes later she switched off the light and made her way upstairs.

There was no sign of Rafael, and she divested her

clothes then slid into bed to sleep within minutes of her head touching the pillow.

At some stage through the night Mikayla felt the drift of fingers over the curve of her hip, and stirred as they trailed to her breast. Lips nuzzled the edge of her shoulder and traced a pattern to her thigh, lingered there, then gently nudged her knee aside to travel an upward path.

No dream could be this vivid, nor was it possible for her skin to feel so acutely sensitised, and she bit back a gasp as Rafael sought to bestow the most intimate kiss of all.

It was a flagrant seduction, and she peaked quickly, roused to a primitive state that knew few bounds, and she cried out, begging for his possession, and huskily castigated him when he didn't give it.

He wanted her hot, passionate, and mindless, and he felt the beat of her fists against his shoulders, caught the desperation as her body arched in supplication. Then he rose up and surged into her, aware of the silken expansion, and he waited until he felt her muscles enclose him, then he began to move, building the rhythm until they were both slick with sensual sweat, and totally *one*.

It took a while to come down, and Mikayla groaned, doubtful of her ability to move.

His mouth covered hers with such gentle evocativeness she almost cried. Was after-play always filled with such languorous sweetness? His touch embraced her with an exquisite fragility, caressing, soothing, until the warmth turned to heat and became fire.

This time the loving was slow, and she died a little, aware deep in her subconscious that she would probably never know his equal.

She slept, and woke at the touch of his hand.

'It's seven thirty,' Rafael informed quietly. He'd already showered, shaved, and was partly dressed. 'I'll go make breakfast.'

Mikayla slid from the bed, gathered fresh underwear and made for the en suite, only to emerge fifteen minutes later dressed in tailored trousers, a long loose knit top that skimmed her thighs, and low-heeled boots. Make-up was minimal, and she ran lightly down the stairs to the kitchen, collected both plates from the servery and carried them to the table before returning for coffee.

Orange juice, scrambled eggs, grilled tomatoes, toast... She forked a mouthful, and sighed. 'You do this very well.'

'Only food, Mikayla?'

She met his musing glance, caught the humorous gleam apparent in those dark eyes, and wrinkled her nose at him. 'That, too.'

He placed a set of keys beside her, together with a remote modem, and a mobile phone. 'The gates,' he indicated. 'Garage, house. As we leave, I'll show you how to programme the alarm system.' He picked up the phone. 'I suggest you give this number to the hospital.'

The mention of hospital had a sobering effect. 'Thank you.'

'I won't be home until around seven.' He finished his coffee, and poured another cup.

'I'll cook dinner. I do a mean Thai chicken curry and rice.'

Rafael reached for his wallet and extracted a note. 'Get what you need.'

Mikayla didn't touch it. 'I have money.' Not much, but enough.

His eyes narrowed. 'Take it.'

'No.' With controlled movements she forked the last mouthful, drained her coffee, then stood to her feet and carried plates to the sink.

He tossed the note down onto the table, and followed her. He'd already washed the skillet, and it took only a minute to stack the plates she rinsed into the dishwasher.

Rafael grabbed his jacket from the chair and shrugged into it, then caught up his briefcase and laptop as she collected her satchel.

When he turned, the note was still on the table.

It was exactly in the same place when he returned home to the tantalising aroma of spicy curry, and bread rolls heating in the oven.

'Do I have time to shower and change?'

'Fifteen minutes,' Mikayla enlightened as she measured rice into gently simmering water. 'I've left the choice of wine to you.'

There was a crisp green salad ready to mix, and the rice, true to her timing, was light and fluffy.

'You're right,' Rafael complimented after the first

few mouthfuls, and she inclined her head. 'What else do you have up your culinary sleeve?'

'Peking duck, prawn risotto, filet mignon, beef bourguignonne... Shall I go on?'

'You took a course in cuisine?'

'My mother loved to cook. I inherited the trait.'

'How was your father today?' He didn't see the need to tell her he received an informed medical update each day.

'The same.'

'And Sammy?'

'He should be out in a day or two.'

Rafael topped up her glass with wine, and filled his own. 'And back into the same environment.'

'He's good at his studies. He's quick, and wants to learn.' I just hope he makes it, she added silently.

'The odds are against him.'

'Not if he fights for it.' She felt fiercely protective, and it showed.

'You intend to see that he does?' Rafael queried with deceptive mildness.

'I intend to try.'

His gaze darkened, and his expression became hard.

'Guardian angels can get shot down.'

'I'm not a babe in the woods where today's youth are concerned,' she bounced back at him.

'Yes,' he refuted silkily, 'you are.'

'No,' she said with measured anger. 'I'm not. Besides, I can take care of myself.'

'Perhaps,' Rafael drawled, 'you'd care to prove that?'

'Any time.'

'In the gym, an hour from now?'

'Okay.'

They took care of the dishes in silence, and afterwards she retrieved textbooks from her satchel, made notes for the next day's lessons, then went upstairs to change into jeans and a top.

Mikayla expected him to be proficient in martial arts. What she didn't bargain for was to have every one of her moves countered and blocked. The session became an exercise in futility...hers.

'Now,' Rafael declared. 'You will learn.'

She had worked up quite a sweat, while *his* breathing hadn't moved up a notch. 'Aren't you afraid I might apply some of the techniques on you in the middle of the night?'

'I'm a very light sleeper,' he assured with a faintly inflected drawl.

'Really?' She wanted to look down her nose at him, but she didn't have the height for it. 'Did you know you snore?'

A husky laugh emerged from his throat. 'Nice try, *pequeña*. Now, are we going to play, or get serious?'

He proceeded to show her tricks that would never be taught in any *dojo*. And he made her repeat them again and again.

An hour later he called a halt, doused the lights, then led her upstairs, filled the spa-bath, and gave her no option but to join him in the pulsing water.

The relaxation therapy would have worked if she'd been alone. Rafael's close proximity merely heightened her senses and made her intensely aware of him...as a man, a lover.

She only had to look at his mouth to vividly recall how it felt on her own, the slide of his tongue, the sensuous curve of his lips as he took her deep, and the passion.

That was the one she had increasing trouble with! She didn't want to admit she enjoyed being in his arms, or the feel of his body against her own, the acute sensation he so easily aroused.

Mikayla knew she had no reason to like him. Even less cause to care. But there was some intrinsic quality that crept beneath her skin and teased her emotions.

Good sex, she attributed. Very good sex. Don't confuse it with anything else.

She meant nothing to him. *Nada*. A new sex toy, nothing more. And like all new toys, they had their use-by date. Just as she would have hers. In fourteen months, the debt would be paid.

Don't get emotionally involved. She repeated it silently, like a mantra.

'The current school semester concludes at the end of this week,' Rafael posed. 'Is that right?'

'Yes. We have a two-week break.'

'I fly to New York on Sunday for several days. You're coming with me.'

Mikayla opened her mouth, then closed it again, and he slanted one eyebrow.

'I trust you have a valid passport?'

'Yes.' *New York.* She strove for calm. 'I didn't realise travelling would be part of the deal.'

His gaze was steady, his expression enigmatic. 'It wasn't specifically mentioned.'

What was that supposed to mean? He *wanted* her with him? *Fool*, she castigated silently.

'You have expressive features,' Rafael observed indolently.

'While yours are a closed book.'

'That bothers you?'

'Yes,' she charged succinctly. 'It gives you an unfair advantage.' She reached forward, caught up a towel, then stood to her feet in one fluid movement and fastened the towel at her breasts.

Rafael let her go, and when he entered the bedroom she was sitting propped up against a nest of cushions, pencil in hand as she made notations from an open textbook onto a legal pad.

Mikayla glanced up as he slid in beside her. 'I need to get this done. If it's going to disturb you, I'll grab a robe and take it downstairs.'

'How long?'

Her brow furrowed. 'Excuse me?'

'How long will it take?' he queried patiently.

'Fifteen minutes, maybe twenty.'

'Twenty,' he conceded. 'Then you get to put the books away.'

Instinct had her lifting the pad to bat him with it, only to find her wrist caught in his.

'Don't try it,' Rafael warned softly, and she threw him a fulminating glare.

'I'll take this downstairs.' She threw aside the bed-covers, only to discover she couldn't move far. 'Let me go.'

'Finish what you're doing.'

'You're impossible!'

'So I've been told,' he relayed imperturbably.

'I could easily…' She faltered, momentarily lost for words.

'What, *pequeña*?'

She turned on him with anger. '*Hit* you!' She managed between clenched teeth, and became further enraged at his soft laughter.

'There are more subtle forms of punishment.'

'You don't possess a *subtle* bone in your body!'

'You're already down four minutes.'

Mikayla bit back a very rude word as she dragged the notepad and textbook into position on her lap and went back to work.

Rafael folded his arms behind his head and watched her. Her pencil moved quickly across the page, and he wondered if she was aware she had a habit of biting her lower lip on occasion.

A strand of her hair fell forward, and he restrained the urge to tuck it behind her ear.

The tee-shirt was going to have to go. A faint smile curved his mouth at the thought of her response should he suggest it.

Any woman of his acquaintance would have packaged her feminine attributes in silk, satin, or worn nothing at all in the need to promote and titillate his interest.

He closed his eyes and focused his mind on the current deal comprising a series of links, which if they all came together, would add considerably to his private wealth.

Mikayla turned the final page of the pertinent chapter intended for the following day's lesson, made a notation in the margin of her pad, then teased her lip with the edge of her teeth. If she used an amusing example to highlight a particularly salient point, the students would retain it. Yes, she decided with satisfaction, that would be the way to go.

She closed the pad, inserted a bookmark at the beginning of the chapter, placed them onto the bedside pedestal, idly checked the time, then she glanced towards the man at her side.

Of all the… She looked at him with a helpless mixture of resignation and indignation. So much for hurrying through her lesson preparation!

His features in repose fascinated her, and she took her time in visually examining the sculpted bone structure, the wide-spaced cheekbones, the strong chin, and lastly, the sensual lines of his mouth.

She could only admire the bunch of biceps, the corded forearms as he lay with his head cupped in his hands, and her gaze strayed to his muscled chest, the whorl of dark hair disappearing beneath the bedcovers.

What would he do, she wondered idly, if she traced a tentative finger over the curve of his mouth?

At that moment his eyes opened, and he regarded her with unblinking solemnity. 'Are you done yet?'

Was he aware she'd been watching him? She hoped not. 'Yes.'

He offered a lazy smile. 'Good.' Then he freed his hands and reached for her, bringing her head down to his as he initiated a kiss that combined gentle evocativeness with the promise of passion.

Would it always be like this? Mikayla agonised as she disregarded restraint and let him have his way with her mouth. The sweet sorcery of his touch swirled into her body, warming the blood, tantalising nerve-ends, until only his possession would ease the vulnerable ache threatening to consume her.

He moved, easing her into a comfortable position, and he took it long and slow, trailing a path to each sensitive pleasure pulse, exploring, until she became a mindless wanton she barely recognised as she begged him for the release she craved.

Afterwards she lay supine, her eyes closed in a bid to still the escaping tears of intense pleasure.

Rafael saw them, and emotion curled round his heart and tugged a little. In an unbidden gesture he traced them with the pads of his fingers, then followed the path with his lips.

CHAPTER SEVEN

SYDNEY in Spring brought the promise of warm weather with clear sunny days, moderate temperatures and a cool breeze off the ocean.

It was a spacious city with sprawling suburbs, the fringes of which hugged the rocky cliffs with expensive and often luxurious real estate. Tall glass-sided buildings rose in varying architectural designed office towers, numerous hotels and apartment buildings, and the city streets hummed with traffic.

The population was very cosmopolitan, with Asian and European residents equalling those of Australian heritage.

Mikayla loved to call it home, for it was here she'd been born and raised, educated and worked.

The ambition to travel overseas had been strong, but studying for a degree had taken time and, although she had ventured to New Zealand and Fiji on holiday with friends, she hadn't had the opportunity to move further afield.

Consequently the prospect of flying to New York was exciting. School and lessons took up much of the daylight hours, followed by visits to her father in hospital each afternoon.

At night, there was Rafael.

She refused to call what they shared *lovemaking*.

Only two people who really cared for each other made *love*. So what was it they had together?

A deal, a tiny voice taunted cynically. You have a *deal. Finis.*

New York was incredible. She loved the fast city pace, the noise from the street, the in-your-face brashness.

The hotel was something else, their suite magnificent, and the service was to die for.

'I'll be tied up in meetings for the rest of the day,' Rafael informed as he checked the electronic mail on his laptop.

Nothing could dampen her spirits. 'I'll go check out the Art Gallery.' She could spend at least a day there, then there was the Museum, and several other places of interest, not to mention the huge department stores.

He tossed her a mobile phone. 'Carry it with you, and use it to contact me.' He cast her a measured look. 'Any time. Take cabs, and don't use the subway. Understood?'

'I've lived in a big city all my life.'

His expression hardened. 'New York isn't Sydney.' He reached for his jacket, extracted his wallet, and handed her a sheaf of notes. 'Use this.'

She stilled. 'I have money.' Holiday salary, which she'd converted to American dollars.

'Take it.'

She looked at him carefully, noting the strength of purpose, the indomitable will. 'I don't need it.'

'*Madre de Dios,*' Rafael swore softly. 'Why must you argue?'

'Why must *you*?' Mikayla countered. 'I'm not a fool. I won't go out of the hotel without adequate money to fund food and cabs.' She drew a breath, and released it slowly. 'If I run short, I'll tell you. Okay?'

He crossed to the wall-safe, opened it, and placed the money inside, then he locked it and handed her a key. 'That makes it easy.'

He was wrong. 'Thank you.'

Rafael checked his watch. 'I have to leave. Are you going to stay here a while, or explore?'

'Explore,' she said without hesitation.

And she did, beginning with a museum.

Rafael rang her on the mobile at midday just as she was biting into a hot dog with mustard and mayo.

There was too much to see and do to waste valuable time sitting over food in a café.

'I should be back at the hotel around five-thirty. We'll go out to dinner,' he relayed without preamble.

'Okay.'

'Where are you?'

'A hot-dog stand.'

There was a moment's pause. 'Where, precisely?'

'Now there you go,' she said with humour. 'I can't see a street name.'

'Mikayla,' he warned in a silky voice, and she cut in before he had a chance to say another word.

'I've got a map. I just haven't looked at it yet.' She

could almost hear him breathe. 'If I get lost, all I have to do is ask someone.' And closed the connection.

He lowered the phone, slid the small unit into his jacket pocket, shook his head, then rejoined three of his associates in the restaurant dining-room...while stifling the urge to forego vintage wine and fine food in favour of sharing a hot dog on a street with a petite blonde.

Mikayla had fun. She walked through Central Park, window-shopped, paused for a cool drink, then rode the subway. It was daylight, dammit, and she fit in just fine, dressed casually in jeans, jumper, and a denim jacket. No one came on to her, nor at any time did she feel threatened, and she emerged onto the platform a few stations down.

Not so good, she observed when she reached street level. The mood was different, in a way she found difficult to explain, and instinct warned against lingering.

Hail a cab, and get out of here was her first thought, but none were within sight. Okay, so she'd go down into the subway and get a train in the direction from whence she came.

It should have been easy, and it would have been if she didn't overshoot the station. Just as she reached street level her phone rang.

There was only one person it could be. 'Rafael?'

'Where in *hell* are you?'

She flinched at the icy anger apparent. 'Precisely?'

'Take a stab at it, Mikayla.'

A cab cruised by, and she hailed it in desperation,

almost beside herself with relief when it pulled in to the kerb. 'I'm about to step into a cab. I'll be at the hotel soon.'

Thirty minutes of stop-and-start traffic, laconic gesturing by the driver accompanied by the occasional cuss word, in a journey that should have taken less than a third of that time. Worse, he charged her by the meter.

She moved into the hotel foyer, summoned a lift, rode it to their designated floor, and seconds later inserted the security card into the door lock.

Rafael was waiting for her, and all it took was one long look from those dark eyes to have the breath stop in her throat.

'Do you have any idea of the time?'

His voice was too quiet. It would almost be more bearable if he'd raised his voice.

'I'm sorry.'

No empty excuses, just an apology, and it didn't come close to appeasing his anger. 'Are you going to enlighten me as to why you're so late?'

'I took a ride on the subway, intending to get off at the next station, and get a cab back to the hotel. Except I misjudged, and went too far.'

'In direct opposition to my request you not ride the subway alone,' he said in a dangerously silky voice, and barely restrained the urge to wring her slender neck at the thought she'd so carelessly chosen just any platform regardless of direction.

'At any time beyond five-thirty, did it occur to you I might be concerned you hadn't returned to the hotel? There was no message at the desk, or on voice-mail, and you didn't answer when I rang your mo-bile.'

'I didn't hear it ring.'

'I'm not surprised.'

'Okay,' she conceded. 'From now on, I'll take cabs.'

'From now on,' Rafael reiterated coolly. 'You'll have a hired limousine at your service to take you wherever you want to go.'

'That's ridiculous.'

He thrust both hands into his trouser pockets. 'It's that, or you stay in the hotel.'

Mikayla looked at him. 'I don't believe this. What right do you have—'

'The right of a man who has paid for your ser-vices.'

It felt as if he'd physically hit her, and pain mo-mentarily clouded her eyes before she was able to control it. 'Of course,' she said quietly. 'How foolish of me to forget.' She moved to the set of drawers, selected fresh underwear, then she made for the en suite. 'It won't take me long to get ready.'

Food wasn't even a consideration, nor was dining in a restaurant a priority. However, anything was bet-ter than staying in their suite.

Mikayla emerged fifteen minutes later, her make-up complete, her hair swept high on top of her head, and she crossed to the wardrobe, selected black silk evening trousers, a black camisole and added a red beaded jacket. Then she slid her feet into stiletto-heeled pumps and caught up her evening purse.

Rafael regarded her steadily, glimpsed the slight tilt of her chin, the coolness apparent in her expressive eyes, and wondered if she had any idea what she'd put him through in the hour he'd paced this suite waiting for her to appear or call.

Mikayla walked to the door, then turned to look at him. 'Shall we leave?'

They rode the lift down in silence, and Rafael led her to the hotel's exclusive a la carte restaurant where the maître d' seated them, then summoned the drinks waiter.

Rafael ordered an excellent pinot noir, then perused the menu. Mikayla selected soup as a starter, with a caesar salad to follow, and incurred Rafael's narrowed glance as she gave the waiter her order.

'Not hungry?'

'No.'

He lifted his wine glass and took a measured swallow. 'Do you intend restricting your conversation to singular responses?'

Mikayla offered him a contrived smile. 'How was your day?' She raised her glass, sipped the superb wine, then looked at him over the rim. 'Did the meeting go well?'

He leaned back in his chair. 'You're in danger of overkill.'

'Really? I thought you wanted pleasant conversation?'

'Let's get this over with, shall we?'

'What, precisely?'

He lifted his glass in a silent salute. 'The argument we're about to have.'

She looked at him carefully. 'I dislike heated public displays.'

'I think we can manage to keep it civilised.'

'There's nothing to discuss,' she said politely, and saw his gaze narrow.

'Yes,' he drawled. 'There is.'

The waiter presented her soup, and placed a seafood starter in front of Rafael.

'No,' she refuted. 'I'm quite clear about your contractual rights to my *services*.' She picked up her spoon, and ignored the thoughtful brooding look he cast her. 'Shall we eat?'

'Your *services* were your suggestion, if you recall?'

'Yes, of course. I apologise for not remembering my position. In future I'll call if I'm running late and, having experienced the New York subway, on my own in daylight, I hereby promise not to repeat the experience. Is that satisfactory?'

'Now you're being facetious,' he drawled, and she dipped her head.

'How perceptive of you to realise that was my intention.'

They finished their starter, and within minutes the waiter delivered the main course.

'Aware of your stubborn streak,' Rafael offered with wry humour, 'I should never have let you loose in the city alone.'

She looked at him, and her eyes held emerald fire. 'I am not stubborn.'

'Yes, you are.'

'No,' she corrected. 'I'm not.'

One eyebrow arched, and his voice was a musing drawl. 'You want to indulge in a game of verbal volleyball?'

'Don't patronise me, dammit!'

His appraisal was slow and deliberate. 'Am I guilty of that?'

'You're treating me like a child.'

'Mikayla,' he offered indolently. 'I give daily thanks that you are anything but a child.'

Comprehension was immediate, and he watched the colour stain her cheeks and settle high across her cheekbones. At the same time her eyes dilated, and her mouth worked at control.

'No comment?'

'I'm still deciding whether that's a compliment or a condemnation.'

'Perhaps you should focus on finishing the meal,' he offered with wry humour.

'I think I've lost my appetite.' She replaced her cutlery and sipped the contents of her glass.

He speared a button mushroom, cut a slice of the superb filet mignon, and offered it to her. 'Try some of this.'

Mikayla looked at the forked morsel of food, then lifted her gaze to meet his, and shook her head.

It was almost eleven when they returned to their

suite, and she slipped off her evening jacket, aware Rafael shrugged out of his own.

Without pausing for thought, she turned and covered the few steps separating them.

'Let me help you.' If she hesitated, she'd be lost! She loosened his tie and freed the top button of his shirt.

'What are you doing?'

'I'm surprised you should ask,' she said evenly as her fingers continued a downward trail until all the buttons were undone. She reached for his belt buckle and undid it. 'Isn't this what a mistress does?'

'Pleasures her—' he paused significantly '—benefactor?'

Mikayla lifted her gaze and met his. 'Yes.'

Rafael's eyes darkened, and she caught a glimpse of something she couldn't define, then it was gone.

'Be my guest.'

His drawling tone strengthened her resolve to play the part she'd offered him so desperately more than three weeks ago.

With deliberate movements she discarded her camisole, then shed the evening trousers. Which left her in bra, briefs, and the stilettos.

The stilettos were a quirk, which gave her the advantage of more than added height, for there was something sophisticated and sexy about stiletto heels. And she needed as much sexy sophistication as she could lay her hands on.

'You're wearing too many clothes,' Mikayla indicated, and heard his husky drawl in response.

'I imagine you intend removing them.'

Oh, yes. 'Shoes and socks,' she bade, and as he lifted each foot she slid them off. The rest was easy, for as soon as she unfastened the zip, his impeccably tailored trousers fell to the carpet. Black silk hipster briefs slid easily over his hips, and he stepped out of both to stand gloriously naked before her. And aroused.

Rafael caught the way her throat moved, and his eyes gleamed. If she wanted to play, he was more than happy to indulge her the game.

She began tentatively, with the tactile pads of her fingers as she traced his ribcage, the muscles covering his chest to the washboard midriff, exploring the hard ridges, teasing the line of hair that arrowed down over his stomach.

His thigh muscles tensed as she curled her fingers into the thick triangle above his groin, and he controlled his breathing as she ran her hands lightly down the inside of each thigh, then slid up to cup him.

The breath hissed between his teeth as she moved higher, stroking him with such a delicate touch it almost drove him to the edge.

Dear God, she thought shakily. Dare she bestow the most intimate kiss of all? Dammit, hadn't he given her that pleasure? Why shouldn't she return the favour?

She wanted to bring him to his knees, sensually, sexually. To have him groan beneath her touch, to lose control and go totally wild...as she did in his arms.

Wasn't that the gift of a mistress? To cater to a man's desires and provide uninhibited pleasure?

It was a mixture of instinct, imagination, driven by a raw primitiveness that soon had him dragging her up against him as he covered her mouth with his own and plundered deep.

Rafael went down onto the bed with her, rolling so she lay beneath him, and he surged in to the hilt, watching as her eyes dilated and she cried out, absorbing him, then he began to move, hard and fast, taking her with him until her body arched high, and everything shattered.

For both of them.

Mikayla felt him shudder, then subside against her as he protected her from his weight and they both fought to bring their ragged breathing under control.

He sought the edge of her neck with his mouth, and kissed her there until she arched her head back, then he nibbled the line of her throat, moving up until he reached her lips where he teased and tantalised with long slow sweeps of his tongue.

Her hands cupped his nape and her fingers slid into his hair, holding his head down to hers as she took the kiss and drove it to a new dimension.

She became so caught up in it, she was hardly aware he rolled onto his back, carrying her with him, and the game became *his* as he held her shoulders firm.

The edge of his teeth grazed the silky globe of her breast to its peak, then suckled, gently at first, then with a sensuality that had her crying out as he took her to the edge between pleasure and pain.

His clever hands created havoc with her senses, teasing where they remained joined until heat became fire, and she lost control. Totally.

Everything splintered and, just when she thought she couldn't bear any more, he drove her towards even greater heights of pleasure.

Afterwards she simply subsided down against him, so completely sated she couldn't move, and she sighed as his arms wrapped around her.

The last thing she remembered was his lips against her temple as she closed her eyes and floated to sleep.

Rafael's meeting was not until two o'clock, and after a leisurely breakfast Mikayla put a call through to the Sydney hospital for a daily report on her father.

He was stable, there was no change, much to her relief.

At nine they took the lift down to the lobby, climbed into the hired limousine and Rafael instructed the driver to tour the inner city.

'This was your home town.' Had to be, Mikayla surmised, for his knowledge was one of easy familiarity.

'Yes.'

'Which part?'

The Bronx, where urban decay was decades old and the streets held ghosts and shadows. It was a lifetime away, yet a memory he would never forget.

'One of the least attractive.' There was everything

in those few words, and nothing. An emptiness that went to the soul.

She heard it, sensed it, and instinctively knew that the man he had become bore few roots of a young boy who'd survived on the streets.

'Let's get out and walk.' She needed to feel the air on her face.

'Central Park, Fifth Avenue,' Rafael instructed.

Afterwards they had lunch in one of the many cafés, then the limousine dropped Rafael outside the building where his meeting was due to take place, and Mikayla had the driver take her to Greenwich Village where she shopped for small gifts to take home.

She returned to the hotel at five, took a shower, and she was in the process of dressing when Rafael entered the suite.

They dined out, returning to Greenwich Village, where the restaurants were many and the night-life vivid and bohemian.

Mikayla adored the atmosphere, and persuaded Rafael to take in a small theatre production before visiting a nearby café.

It was magical, and she loved the days, the sightseeing. Rafael was able to spend the occasional morning with her, and together they took the Staten Island ferry, explored the botanical gardens. Each evening they dined out, visited the cinema, the theatre.

The nights were something else, and with each passing one she became more aware of her own traitorous emotions, and needs.

There was a sense of completeness she'd never

thought to achieve, a sensual knowledge that flowered deep within and brought with it a generosity of mind, body and soul.

Don't give him your heart, a tiny voice warned, and she ignored it, sure of her ability to control her emotions.

The day of their departure arrived all too soon, and they flew in to Sydney early Sunday morning, arriving home to shower, change and unpack.

Mikayla drove to the hospital and visited with her father. He looked tired, and his colour had changed...or was that because she hadn't seen him for a week?

It unsettled her, and after she left she stopped by the Rocks, spent half an hour with Maisie, then she drove to Woollahra.

Rafael was in the study, keying data into the computer, and he took one look at her pale features, the dark bruising beneath her eyes, and closed everything down.

'Bed, I think,' he said quietly.

'I'm not tired.'

'Yes, you are.'

'No, I'm not.'

He lifted her easily into his arms and carried her upstairs to their room, then he discarded his own clothes, removed hers, and drew her beneath the bedcovers.

He was warm and solid and alive, and she only made a token protest when he pulled her close against him.

'Sleep,' he bade, and she did. Long and deeply, waking just before dawn.

It was then they made love. Slowly, and with such exquisite care, she almost wanted to weep.

CHAPTER EIGHT

SCHOOL brought a return to reality and a daily routine that saw Sammy back in class. Teenage bravado was a badge, and he wore it well, causing Mikayla to regard him with a mixture of hidden amusement and despair.

The last semester of the year tended to be fraught with preparation for major exams, and it increased the stress levels for students and teachers alike.

One day seemed to blend into another as she dedicated her time to classes, visited her father each afternoon, and joined the social circuit with Rafael.

Her appearance as his partner caused a degree of speculation and, while no one dared question Rafael Velez-Aguilera's choice of female companion, there was evident curiosity as to her background and social standing.

Zilch, in comparison to the social elite attending a private dinner party given by one of the city's society doyennes known for her devotion to raising money for charity, Mikayla reflected a few weeks later as she stood at Rafael's side making polite conversation.

'And what is it you do?'

'I teach English literature to students,' she responded politely.

'How interesting. One of the private schools, I presume?'

'State,' Mikayla corrected, and saw the woman's eyes narrow fractionally.

Rafael Velez-Aguilera commanded respect, he donated large sums to charity. He must, at all costs, be humoured.

Mikayla could almost see the wheels turning, and felt mildly amused.

At that moment he turned, caught her expression, and leaned towards her. 'Another drink?'

'I really don't think so,' she said solemnly.

'Something amuses you?'

'The charity's funding objective for the year would be achieved in one hit if all the women present donated the jewellery they're wearing.'

'Perhaps you could make the suggestion.'

She cast him a steady look. 'And cause an outrage? I don't think so.'

Speaking of which, a late entry into this soiree was none other than the beautiful Sasha, *clinging* like a sinuous vine to a male partner.

A deliberate set-up, Mikayla attributed, admiring Sasha's acting ability. The target was Rafael, jealousy the weapon.

It didn't appear to work, and Mikayla almost felt sorry for her as they sat down to dinner.

The table was long, the setting elaborate, with fine bone china, gleaming silver cutlery, and crystal glasses assembled in sets to accommodate an assortment of vintage wines.

Accident or design? Or had Sasha pre-arranged to be seated beside Rafael? Mikayla assured herself she didn't care.

Uniformed staff served a delectable five-course meal, during which Mikayla conducted an interesting conversation with the man seated next to her on government education funding and the scholastic system.

It helped her ignore the deliberately subtle gestures Sasha initiated. Elegant hands with their lacquered nails which rested from time to time on Rafael's arm. The sultry smile, the husky laughter, the feline purr in her voice.

Rafael was at his charming best, solicitous, and Mikayla responded with reciprocal affection. Playing a part, she accorded silently.

'A little more wine?'

She cast Rafael a steady look, glimpsed the faint gleam apparent in those dark eyes, and wanted to hit him. He was amused, damn him.

It was easy to offer him a smile, and she placed a hand on his thigh, clenched her nails against hard muscle, then lightly stroked her fingers towards his groin.

'No, thank you.'

'Careful, *pequeña*,' he warned softly.

She deliberately widened her eyes. 'I don't know what you mean.'

'I wonder if you'll be quite so brave when we're alone,' he offered silkily, and saw fearlessness replace playful humour.

'Count on it.'

'You would challenge me?'

'No one else appears to do so.'

'And you think it might be good for me,' Rafael mocked, watching the expressive play of emotions chase her features.

'Yes,' she said simply, and wondered at his smile.

Coffee was served in a large entertainment room, and it was there the true purpose of the evening began with numerous interesting items put up to auction.

Paintings, objets d'art, jewellery. It was an eclectic mix, and the bidding process intrigued her, for it appeared it wasn't so much the item itself but who could and would outbid *who*.

'See anything you like?' Rafael queried, and she indicated a small Pro Hart painting depicting a simple scene on display.

'When it comes up, bid.' He mentioned a limit, and she cast him a startled glance.

'Are you serious?'

'I wouldn't suggest it, otherwise.'

Mikayla watched with renewed interest, and when the painting came up she went in at the first offer. Sasha followed with the second, and as the bidding rose so did the guests' speculation, for it became obvious they were witnessing a private war.

The charity is a worthy cause, Mikayla repeated silently as the bidding rose in one-hundred-dollar increments. Rafael can well afford it. However, she refused to go above the limit he'd set, just as she avoided glancing towards Sasha as the auctioneer did his closing spiel.

'Going once, twice—'

'One thousand.'

There was a collective hush at Rafael's bid, and Mikayla watching with mounting disbelief as Sasha took up a personal challenge to win.

No one was in any doubt it was a battle between the ex-girlfriend and the mistress.

'Three thousand. Going once, twice…sold.' To Rafael Velez-Aguilera.

'Was that meant to prove something?' Mikayla demanded quietly, and met Rafael's amused glance.

'Yes, I believe so.'

'Did it have to be done so *publicly*?'

'You admired the painting. I bought it. The money goes to charity. End of story.'

'No,' she said simply. 'It's not.'

'Your reasoning fascinates me,' he drawled.

'Congratulations, darling.'

They both turned as one at the familiar sound of Sasha's dulcet tones.

'A pretty little piece. I hope Mikayla appreciates it.'

'I'm flattered,' Mikayla ventured with studied politeness, and glimpsed Sasha's moue.

'Rafael is very indulgent, aren't you, *querido*?'

She turned to the man at her side, and performed an introduction. 'Enrico Alvarez.'

Enrico leaned forward, took hold of Mikayla's hand, lifted it to his lips, and lingered a fraction too long. 'Charmed.'

Mikayla offered a polite smile, and withdrew her

hand. Rafael merely inclined his head in acknowl-
edgement. The tension apparent was stifling, and with
a murmured excuse she slipped out the door and
sought the guest powder room.

Five minutes later she emerged into the hallway to
discover Sasha waiting with contrived patience a few
feet distant.

'There you are. Rafael expressed concern at your
absence.'

'Really?'

'I haven't figured out what your attraction is, but
it must be quite something to capture Rafael.'

'Perhaps the sex is good?'

Sasha's gaze hardened. 'Don't be too smug, darling.'

'The word isn't in my vocabulary.' She drew a
shallow breath. 'If there's a point to this ambush,
you'd do well to get to it.'

'Enrico is fascinated with you.'

This was unbelievable. 'You're offering me Enrico
as a trade for Rafael?'

'Enrico is rich, and charming,' Sasha qualified.

'And as long as the cash flows…?' Mikayla trailed,
and saw Sasha's catlike smile.

'I see we understand each other.'

'No,' she refuted quietly. 'We don't.'

'Then you won't play?'

'Not any game on your list.' She moved past Sasha,
traversed the hallway, then re-entered the entertainment room.

Rafael watched as Mikayla crossed towards him.

There was something about her that curled around his heart and tugged a little. He felt the familiar stirring in his loins as desire flared, and his gaze became slightly hooded as he glimpsed Enrico Alvarez move into her path.

Jealousy? It wasn't an emotion that sat well, and he dismissed it as Mikayla offered Enrico a polite smile, executed a neat sidestep and continued across the room.

'Can I get you some more coffee?' he offered as she reached his side.

'Something stronger?' Mikayla quizzed.

His lips curved into a lazy smile. 'Let me guess. Sasha chose to say a few words.'

She flicked him a telling glance. 'I was not amused.'

'The auction is almost over.'

'Then we can leave?'

A husky chuckle emerged from his throat. 'Your eagerness to go home overwhelms me.'

'It's a question of choices,' she alluded cynically.

He slid a hand to her nape and gently massaged the tense muscles there. 'Ten minutes, *pequeña*.'

Rafael waited until they were in the car and clear of their hosts' street. 'Want to tell me about it?'

Mikayla could see little of his expression in the darkness. 'Wealth has its own rules.'

'Elucidate.'

'Well now, let me see. Two rich men, two women. Does it really matter who is paired with *who*? Sasha was a mite peeved I wasn't willing to oblige.'

She cast him a quick glance, caught the movement of his mouth in the light of a passing car, and retreated to frigid restraint. 'It's not funny.'

If he laughed, she'd hit him. Except he didn't, and she remained silent for the rest of the short drive home.

Rafael let her precede him into the house, and watched the set of her shoulders, her straight back, as she ascended the stairs ahead of him.

Mikayla undressed in silence, removed her make-up, brushed her teeth more vigorously than usual, then she pulled on her tee-shirt and emerged into the bedroom to discover Rafael already in bed.

He was leaning back against the pillows, his chest bare, the sheet at his waist, and she slid in, then studiously turned on her side away from him.

Seconds later she heard the click of the lamp and the room was plunged into darkness.

Mikayla didn't move, and she deliberately steadied her breathing, forcing herself to relax as she mentally counted off the minutes. Two, three, four... Ten, eleven, twelve. Twenty.

Dammit. Why was her imagination in overdrive? And so focused on the man who slept within touching distance?

Admit it, a tiny voice taunted. You want him. *Need* the slow slide of his hands on your body. The feel of his mouth as it wrought its own havoc.

Evocative images tantalised her mind, and she shifted tentatively, stretching a leg as if restless in sleep. Maybe if she let a hand drift a little—

'All played out?'

Mikayla froze as hands slid beneath her slender frame and lifted her over him.

He cupped her nape, pulled her head down to his, and took possession of her mouth in a kiss that plundered deep and long as his hands shaped her back, her buttocks, then slid her into a sitting position astride him.

In one primitive movement he arched her high, then brought her down, heard her groan as her muscles stretched to accommodate him, and rocked gently back and forth until she caught his rhythm.

It was all she could do to hang on as he rode her hard, and she gasped as he caught her close and rolled so their positions were reversed.

Dear God. Each time they came together, she didn't think it could be *more*, but somehow it was. She arched up against him, and cried out as his mouth sought one delicate peak, suckled, then rolled the sensitive tip between the edge of his teeth.

Sensation shuddered through her body, and her hands kneaded his shoulders, caressed, then slid round his nape as she dragged his head up to hers, possessing his mouth with such raw hunger she lost track of time and place until there was only the man, the moment, and the passion.

It was a long time before they both subsided into a drifting after-play where the tracing pads of his fingers soothed her cooling flesh, and his lips trailed sensual warmth to the curve of her neck, the soft swell of her breast.

*   *   *

It had been a week since Joshua's transfer into a private room, and when Mikayla had queried why, the reason given was straightforward...Rafael Velez-Aguilera's instructions.

'You would prefer your father to die with dignity in the privacy of his own room?' Rafael queried coolly when she demanded an explanation.

'Yes, but—'

He'd simply brushed a hand over her cheek and pressed her lips closed. 'No *but, pequeña.* I will take care of it.'

Something else for which she'd be beholden to him. She'd kept a list of clothes he'd insisted she have. When she left him, she intended to repay as much as she could afford in reparation. It was a matter of pride, *hers.*

The hospital visits began to take their toll, emotionally, for Joshua seemed to become more frail with each passing day, and it broke her heart when she walked into his room one Monday to discover he was on oxygen and slipping in and out of consciousness.

Mikayla didn't want to leave him, and she located the head nurse, asked pertinent questions, then retreated to a designated area for mobile use and put a call through to Rafael.

Seconds later he came on the line, his voice low against the faint hum of background noise. 'Problems?'

She'd interrupted a meeting, and she offered a swift apology. 'It's Joshua.' She didn't need to say more. 'I'd like to stay a while.'

Rafael checked his watch, and made a few adjustments to his schedule. 'Keep in touch.'

'Yes.' She broke the connection, and stood staring sightlessly at the colourful wall poster a few feet away.

She'd known of this outcome for months, but nothing could have prepared her for the moment her father would actually slip from this world.

Slowly she turned, retraced her steps to Joshua's room, and sat holding his hand.

It was there Rafael found her an hour later, he who organised the food sent in, and he who remained by her side until just before midnight when Joshua slipped away from them.

Rafael led her from the room, turned her into his arms and simply held her.

She couldn't cry, there was just a consuming numbness, and after a few minutes she lifted her head and moved back a pace. 'I'm all right.'

She was far from all right. Her features were pale and her eyes bore a haunted look he would give anything to diminish.

He dealt with formalities, then put her into his car and drove her home, ran the spa-bath, collected a bottle of chilled wine and two glasses, gently divested her clothes, his own, then he stepped into the bath and drew her back against him.

'Want to talk?' Rafael queried quietly as he brushed his lips to her hair, and she shook her head, grateful for the comfort he offered.

Later, towelled dry, she didn't protest when he slid into bed and pulled her close.

The following few weeks possessed an unreal quality as Mikayla threw herself into her work. She planned elaborate meals which involved extensive preparation and Rafael observed her increasingly pale features, the loss of weight, decided enough was enough, made a few phone calls, and ensured he was home when she walked in the door the following afternoon.

Mikayla looked at him in startled surprise. 'You're home early.'

She looked fragile, and he thrust hands into his trouser pockets in a bid to stop himself from hauling her into his arms.

'We're taking a flight to the Gold Coast for the weekend.'

Her eyes widened. 'You're kidding, right?'

'No. We're due at the airport an hour from now.'

'We can't just pick up and leave at a moment's notice,' she protested.

'Yes,' he drawled, 'we can.' He turned towards the stairs. 'Now, do you pack for you, or shall I? Your choice.'

'*Why?*'

He was already ascending the stairs, and he didn't pretend to misunderstand. 'Do you need a specific reason?'

'Yes, dammit!' She followed him, anger mounting with every step she took.

Anger he could handle. It was the flat nerveless

demeanour she'd displayed since Joshua's death that got to him.

They reached the bedroom, and there on the long footstool stood two holdalls, one packed, the other empty.

'I don't want to go anywhere.'

'Procrastinating won't prove a thing.'

Mikayla threw him a venomous glare. 'I don't think I like you very much.'

Rafael crossed to her walk-in robe, opened it and began riffling through the contents.

'I have a thick skin, *pequeña*. Hate me as much as you like.'

She watched in disbelief as he tossed clothes onto the bed, then followed it with underwear. 'What do you think you're doing?'

'We leave the house in ten minutes.'

She moved quickly to the walk-in robe and batted her hands against his. 'Damn you. I'll do it!' Minutes later she had restored the clothes he'd selected back onto hangers and into drawers, then made her own selection.

'It would help if you told me whether this trip is business or strictly relaxation.'

'Relaxation,' Rafael informed indolently.

Quick deft movements had her folding everything into the holdall. 'You're the most maddening, *determined* man I've ever had the misfortune to meet.'

'*Misfortune*, Mikayla?' His voice was pure silk, and ripped the anger from her in seconds.

'That isn't strictly true,' she admitted quietly.

'*Gracias*,' he acknowledged wryly, watching as she collected toiletries, basic make-up and thrust them into the holdall.

They made the airport with minutes to spare and were among the last to board a flight which took just over an hour before it touched down at Coolangatta.

Rafael picked up a hire car and it was dark as they drove thirty kilometres north to the coastal tourist strip.

Tall high-rise apartment buildings and hotels appeared like illuminated sentinels lining the gently curved foreshore, and Rafael drove through Main Beach to the Sheraton Mirage Resort, a low-rise architectural masterpiece built right on the ocean.

Their suite was spacious with a view to die for, and there was champagne on ice, flowers, fresh fruit and chocolates in welcome.

'Decadent,' Mikayla accorded with a musing smile as she stood looking out over the huge lagoon with its island bar and walkways.

There was some colour in her cheeks, Rafael saw with relief, and just her smile was sufficient reward for the rescheduling he'd had his secretary organise to free up this particular weekend.

'Can we wander out there a while?'

The champagne could wait. 'If that's what you want.'

She turned towards him. 'Are you pandering to me?'

'Indulging,' he drawled, and the edges of her mouth lifted.

'That could be dangerous.'

'Plan on it.'

'I think we should go for that walk,' she said solemnly, and a husky chuckle emerged from his throat as he crossed to the door.

The cool evening air feathered her skin as they emerged out onto the lagoon area, and she didn't protest when he caught hold of her hand and threaded his fingers between her own.

They crossed towards the oceanfront, and wandered along the sandy foreshore until the floodlit area ceased, then they retraced their steps, re-entered the hotel lobby, and took the footbridge crossing the road to the Marina.

There were restaurants, café's, boutiques, and immediately adjacent the stylish Palazzo Versace where little expense had been spared to complete its luxurious design.

They took time out for a liqueur coffee in an outdoor café, and viewed the Marina with its many cruisers at individual moorings.

The area held an ambience that was both trendy and casual, as well as being popular if the number of people present was any indication.

Mikayla could feel some of the tension begin to dissipate. The sea air, perhaps? The prospect of two whole days in Rafael's company uninterrupted by the call of anything remotely connected to business? Nothing on the social calendar?

Surf, sun and sand, she mused, and felt pleasure stir at the thought.

Rafael surveyed her in open appraisal. The knot of silken hair atop her head was beginning to slip, and he restrained the urge to lean forward and free the remaining pins.

He wanted to cup her delicate features and touch his mouth to her own, linger a little, savour, then slide his tongue into that sweet cavern and take possession in a prelude to intimacy.

At that moment Mikayla glanced towards him, and he watched her eyes widen, viewed the soft tinge of pink that coloured her cheeks with musing indulgence and felt something curl round his heart, tug, then tighten as she offered a tentative smile.

'You're tired,' Rafael said gently, and saw one eyebrow lift.

'I am?'

'Definitely.'

His lazy tone didn't fool her in the slightest.

'Somehow I get the feeling that while bed is an option, sleep isn't?'

He reached out a hand and brushed his knuckles across her cheek. 'Eventually.'

Rafael eased his lengthy frame from the chair in one fluid movement, then he leaned forward and drew her to her feet. His gaze held the promise of passion, and something else. 'I undertake to do all the work.'

Mikayla swallowed the lump that had suddenly risen in her throat. 'Well, then. That's a relief.'

Surely, she pondered dreamily much later, intimacy didn't get much better than this. He had the touch, the skill, the knowledge to drive a woman wild.

A slow stroke of his fingers, that sensuous mouth, and she went up in flames.

He may have started it, she reflected on the edge of sleep, but she'd finished it. Gloriously, exulting in a mutual orgasm that took them high and tipped them over the edge. She heard him groan an instant before his mouth cut off her cries, and together their bodies convulsed, then shuddered with the heat of passion so intense she doubted she'd ever experience its equal.

Mikayla slept, only to stir as skilled fingers stroked and probed, and she went up and over, arching into him as he suckled her breast, tantalising its tender peak until she cried out.

Then he trailed his lips up the curve of her throat, lingered there, then moved to possess her mouth in a kiss that stole the breath from her body.

In one smooth movement he rolled onto his back, carrying her with him to straddle his hips, and she smiled in the early dawn light as she took her turn to tease and tantalise before taking him deep inside, riding him hard until the breath hissed through his teeth.

Afterwards he cradled her close, and smoothed the tumbled hair from her face.

'I hope,' Mikayla ventured slowly, 'you don't have plans for anything adventurous for another few hours.'

'No vigorous walk along the beach? A swim in the lagoon? An early morning set of tennis?' Rafael teased as he brushed his lips to her temple.

'Room service breakfast at eight,' she pleaded, and felt the drift of his fingers as they traced her spine.

'Eight-thirty,' he enlightened as he sought the soft curve at the edge of her neck with his lips, nuzzled there, then moved to her shoulder.

'Good.' She closed her eyes, unaware that Rafael lay awake watching her as she slept.

Mikayla woke to the sound of the doorbell as the porter delivered their breakfast, and she pulled on a robe as Rafael set everything out on the table.

He'd slid open the drapes and there was a clear view out over the ocean.

Orange juice, cereal, toast and aromatic coffee, and she sipped the first, added fruit to the second, and lingered over toast and more coffee while Rafael did justice to bacon, eggs, and tomatoes.

Afterwards they showered, explored the Palazzo Versace hotel complex opposite, then returned to the Sheraton to stretch out on loungers beneath a shade umbrella by the lagoon.

It was wonderfully relaxing, Mikayla reflected as her gaze drifted over the lagoon waters. There was a peaceful sense of isolation and timelessness, aided by the expanse of the adjacent ocean. She could close her eyes and imagine they were at the edge of the world.

CHAPTER NINE

'Do you want to eat lunch here, or venture to nearby Tedder Avenue?'

The sound of Rafael's drawling tones brought her into a sitting position, and she lowered her sunglasses.

'I get to choose?' She didn't need to think. 'Tedder Avenue.'

It had changed since she last visited, and was now a trendy café area where the social elite lingered over coffee and viewed the passing parade of equally upwardly mobile people.

The Gold Coast promoted a laid-back casual lifestyle far removed from the hype and hustle of a big commercial city.

Tuscan-style apartment buildings vied with Greek, Caribbean, French provincial, in varying colours and each bearing exotic names. Then there were the magnificent riverside mansions, the meandering Nerang River, and the white sandy beaches.

It was, she reflected, a wonderful place to play.

Rafael chose a restaurant where seafood was a speciality, and they both indulged in small servings of sautéed prawns, oysters kilpatrick, and succulent lobster served with a variety of salad greens.

Rafael ordered champagne, a superb Dom

Perignon, chilled to perfection, and Mikayla wrinkled her nose at him as the aerated bubbles fizzed.

'Are we celebrating?'

He touched the rim of his flute to her own. 'Life.' His mouth curved into a musing smile. 'Isn't that a celebration in itself?'

Yes, she acknowledged silently, aware he had cleverly initiated this weekend with just that purpose in mind.

For a while she got to share his. Then they'd part and go their separate ways, and for her, life would never be the same.

Would she, when the time came, be able to move easily away from him?

Why did the mere thought tear at something deep inside and cause her pain?

Each day, each night in his arms, made the prospect of parting a little harder, for there was an intrinsic need she was afraid only he could fill.

It was more than just sex. It was part of her heart, her soul, everything that she was…and more.

Could it be *love*?

Dear God. She was just being fanciful, allowing her emotions to rule her brain.

Wasn't she?

To fall in love with Rafael Velez-Aguilera was akin to jumping off the edge of a cliff. Survival wouldn't be an option.

When she left, it would be the hardest thing she'd ever have to do.

And Rafael? Could he move on to someone else

without a second thought? Any number of women would queue to take her place, and Sasha would take the lead.

Why, within a few weeks he'd probably forget Mikayla Petersen's existence!

'More champagne?'

She glanced at her empty flute, and couldn't recall finishing the contents. 'Please.'

She rarely had more than a single glass, and Rafael's eyes narrowed thoughtfully as he refilled both flutes.

After lunch Rafael suggested a drive through the hinterland, and they took one route up to Mount Tamborine, explored a few craft shops, lingered over a drink at one of the few quaint café's, then returned to the Coast via Canungra.

It was dark when they arrived back at the hotel, and they showered, dressed, then wandered across the footbridge to the Marina complex to dine in a restaurant famed for its cuisine.

Together they lingered, enjoying the wine, the food, the tranquil view, until almost eleven, when they returned to their hotel suite and indulged in a long sweet loving that almost made her weep with the joy of it.

Sunday they rose late, went downstairs for a leisurely brunch, then lay on loungers beneath one of many sun umbrellas lining the lagoon. Afterwards they took one of the canal cruises through some of the waterways and returned in time to change, pack and drive to the airport for the evening return flight to Sydney.

It had been a wonderful weekend, and exactly what she'd needed, Mikayla reflected as the jet took its southward path.

'Thank you.'

Rafael took her hand and lifted it to his lips. 'My pleasure.'

He waited until dawn to reveal he was taking the early morning flight for the first of several meetings in Melbourne, Adelaide, Brisbane and Perth.

'How long will be you be away?' Mikayla queried as he held her close after a tumultuous loving that left her weak-willed and trembling.

'Three, possibly four days.' He brushed his lips against hers, lingered, savoured, then drifted to settle at her temple. 'Miss me.'

Oh, yes, she would that. Every day, every night. Dear Lord, especially the nights.

'Maybe,' she qualified, then cried out in protest as his teeth nipped her earlobe. 'That hurt.'

'It was meant to.'

She retaliated with a love bite close to one male nipple, and gasped as he rolled onto his back and drew her over him.

'You want to play?'

His mouth hovered far too close to her breast, and she pressed her lips against his forehead, teased a path down the slope of his nose, then angled her mouth to take possession of his own.

'I think,' she murmured when she raised her head. 'You should conserve your energy.'

His husky laughter was almost her undoing, and he surprised her with a brief hard kiss. 'Ah, concern for my well-being,' he mused. 'How touching.' He smoothed a hand over her slender curves, playfully patted her bottom, then shifted her onto the bed. 'Time for me to hit the shower, dress, and drive to the airport.'

She was asleep when he emerged, and she didn't stir as he quietly dressed. He paused for a moment, crossed to the bed, and stood looking at her as she hugged the pillow. For a moment he almost regretted having to leave. He leaned down and gently brushed a swathe of hair from her cheek, then he turned and walked from the room.

Mikayla told herself she enjoyed the freedom of being totally in charge of her life during Rafael's absence. All it took was the first night alone in the bed they shared to prove her wrong.

Dammit, she missed being held in his arms, the feel of his warm body curved against her own. She missed the sex. But worst of all, she missed *him*.

Consequently she spent a restless night, and woke the next morning determined to minimise the effect of his absence.

A phone call to Maisie and an invitation to stay over took care of Tuesday evening, and she'd promised Sammy a restaurant meal if he scored high marks in his pre-exam tests...which he had, and she made a mental note to issue the invitation for Wednesday evening. That left Thursday. Maybe Maisie and a few mutual friends could make up a party and go to the movies.

Between school, marking and setting lesson, and an active social life, she wouldn't have time to *think* about the dynamic man who had managed to slip beneath her skin and invade her heart.

Tuesday afternoon Mikayla entered the supermarket, collected a trolley, and began stocking it with items on her list. The main staples filled the refrigerator and pantry, but she'd run out of milk, bread, and she needed to stock up on fresh fruit and vegetables for the dish she planned to cook for dinner.

It was almost five when she entered the house, and she discarded her satchel, took the groceries through to the kitchen, and began preparations.

Maisie buzzed from the gate at six, and Mikayla wiped her hands, pressed the release mechanism, then walked to the front door.

'*Wow*. This is like—real class,' Maisie declared as she entered the main foyer. 'Do I get to have a tour?'

'Sure, why not? After dinner?' she suggested. 'Let's have a glass of wine, then we'll eat, and I'll show you around.'

It was nice to sit and chat with the ease of long friendship. The food was good, and she acknowledged Maisie's praise with a quick smile.

'You love him, don't you?'

The query came out of the blue, and it took Mikayla a moment to find her voice. 'Pass.'

'Hey, it's me, Maisie, remember?'

Mikayla stood to her feet and began collecting plates and cutlery.

'You wouldn't be here with him if you didn't care.'

True friendship had its disadvantages. The friend didn't hold back, and knew you too well. 'I'm trying to come to terms with it,' she said quietly. Wasn't that the truth!

The house, the grounds, earned Maisie's approval, and afterwards they drank coffee, watched two videos, then went to bed late.

Mikayla had trouble sleeping, and she woke at dawn, rose, showered and dressed, then she went downstairs, opened her satchel and dealt with the day's curriculum.

Rafael hadn't phoned, but then she hadn't expected him to. She had his mobile number, and she could easily call. But what the hell would she say? *I miss you?*

'Hi, you're up early.'

She glanced up, met Maisie's bright features, and offered a reciprocal smile. 'Coffee's hot.' She slid everything into her satchel, and quickly set the table. 'What do you feel like for breakfast?'

Maisie filled two mugs from the steaming carafe. 'Whatever you're having.'

'How about we go to the movies Thursday evening?' Mikayla broached over cereal and fruit, and met Maisie's quick grin.

'Missing him, huh?'

'Yes.'

'Okay. We get to eat first, right? I choose the café, you choose the movie?'

'Done.'

Half an hour later they each slid into separate cars and followed each other down the driveway.

It was important to Sammy that no one at school knew his English literature teacher was taking him out to dinner. Consequently he studiously strove for normality during class.

Mikayla had made arrangements to meet him in the city immediately inside the restaurant venue. He'd insisted he take the train in, and flatly refused to allow her to collect him at home.

The phone rang just as she finished dressing, and she picked up the bedroom extension.

'Mikayla.'

The sound of Rafael's voice wove round her nerve-ends and tugged. 'Hi.'

'Any problems?'

'Everything is fine.' Heavens, get a grip! 'Where are you?'

'Perth. All being well, I'll be on the afternoon flight, Friday.'

'Okay.'

'Just…*okay*, Mikayla?'

She heard the humour in his voice, and retaliated in kind. 'The house is lonely without you.'

His husky laughter did strange things to her equilibrium. 'I'm tempted to insist you take the morning flight and join me here.'

'I have a job, remember?'

'You could take sick leave.'

'No,' she refuted. 'I couldn't.'

'Don't plan anything Friday night.'

Her heart quickened to a faster beat. 'Okay.'

'Your vocabulary needs work,' Rafael drawled indolently. 'Although *talking* isn't what I have in mind. Goodnight, *pequeña*.'

She needed a moment to dispel the wildly erotic images teasing her brain. Then she caught up her purse, slid her feet into heeled pumps, and went downstairs to the car.

Sammy was waiting when she entered the restaurant, and she successfully hid her surprise. He looked older than his sixteen years, and he'd gone to some trouble with his clothes, for the jeans were black dress jeans, the shirt was done up and he wore a tie, a leather jacket, and his hair was groomed into a stylish ponytail.

'You look great,' Mikayla greeted, and restrained herself from embarrassing him with a brief hug.

'You, too.'

'Shall we go straight to the table?'

The maître d' joined them, and it was Sammy who confirmed the booking. She wanted to say *well done*, but didn't dare.

When they were seated, he perused the wine list, consulted her for a suggestion, then ordered a chardonnay. The menu received similar attention, and her eyes twinkled a little as she gave him her selection and requested he order.

'I want to thank you for doing this for me,' he said with sincerity. 'No other teacher would bother.' His gaze was steady. 'So, why did you?'

'Because I believe in you.'

'Maybe, if we keep in touch, when I graduate I can get to take *you* out to dinner?'

'I'd like that very much,' she said gently.

They had almost finished the main course when an attractive couple drew level with their table.

'Mikayla?'

She glanced up at the sound of that feminine voice and saw Sasha, with Enrico in tow. It was difficult to credit, with all the fine restaurants in Sydney, their choice had coincided.

'Sasha, Enrico,' she greeted politely, and indicated her guest. 'Sammy D'alvecchio.'

'This is a surprise, darling. I thought Rafael was away?'

'Yes, he is.'

Sasha flicked Sammy a glance, then settled on Mikayla's features. 'Enjoy.'

'You don't like her,' Sammy said quietly the instant Sasha and Enrico were out of earshot.

'Did it show?'

'No. But then, I get to read your expression every day in class.'

'That bad, huh?'

'You're the best teacher I've ever had. Anyone gives you trouble, just let me know.'

'Thank you,' she declared solemnly.

They ordered dessert, lingered over coffee, and it

was well after ten when she took care of the bill and they emerged onto the pavement.

'I'll drive you home.'

'I'll get the train.'

'Sammy—'

'You know I live in a bad part of town. I don't want you driving away from there alone at night. *Capisce*?'

'In that case, let me drive you to the station.'

'I'll walk you to your car.' His gaze was steady, with a knowledge far beyond his years. 'Then I'll walk to the station.'

She wanted to argue, but knew it was pointless. Almost as if he knew, he touched her hand. 'I can handle myself.'

It took five minutes, and she slid in behind the wheel, then rolled down the window. 'Take care.'

His smile was quick, warm. 'You, too. And thanks, for tonight.'

She waited until he moved out of sight, then she urged the Mini out of the car park and drove home.

The message light was blinking on the answering machine when she entered the house, and she pressed the appropriate button.

'Mikayla, darling.' The recorded voice was feminine. '*Sasha*. Loved your toy-boy, sweetie. Although I doubt Rafael will be amused.'

And you can't wait to tell him, Mikayla thought, wanting to be there to witness Sasha's expression when she discovered the supposed *toy-boy* was a six-teen-year-old school student.

Sleep proved elusive, and she woke to the sound of the digital alarm, rose, showered, ate a quick breakfast, then drove to school to spend an uneventful day in class.

Maisie rang during the lunch break to confirm arrangements for dinner and the movies, and they met at a trendy café within walking distance of a major cinema complex, ordered, then took time over a casual meal.

The movie was a Jane Austen classic with a feisty heroine. It had a beautiful setting, the acting was superb, and the dialogue witty. They both loved every minute, and emerged laughing over one particular high spot on film.

'Coffee?' Maisie queried, and Mikayla acquiesced, not wanting the evening to end too soon.

'Why not?'

They chose a café, ordered, then lingered until almost midnight before departing for their individual homes.

Friday dawned bright and clear, and Mikayla felt as if every hour dragged. *The afternoon flight* had little relevance when she didn't even know which airline he was travelling on, and she drove home unsure whether he'd be there or not.

Not, she discovered, and contained her disappointment as she went through to the kitchen, retrieved the apricot chicken casserole she'd prepared that morning and slipped it into the microwave.

It was crazy to feel so wound up, she chided mentally as she made her way to the bedroom to shower and change.

All day she'd been aware of an increasing degree of nervous tension, and the thought of what the night would bring sent heat coursing through her veins.

Mikayla stripped off her clothes and walked naked into the en suite, adjusted the water temperature, then entered the shower stall.

She shampooed her hair, rinsed off the suds, then she caught up the soap and began smoothing it over her body.

'Why don't you let me do that?'

CHAPTER TEN

MIKAYLA felt the soap slip from her fingers at the sound of that familiar drawl, and her eyes widened as Rafael stepped in beside her.

'You're home,' she managed unsteadily, and bit back a gasp as he cupped her face, then fastened his mouth over her own in a kiss that was all heat and possession as he took her deeper with passion and desire.

His hands slid over her shoulders, then down her back as he caught her close, and she leaned in against him, exulting in the strength of his arousal.

A hand shaped her buttocks, then curved inwards as his fingers slid skilfully to probe the moist silken part of her that responded so well to his touch.

He felt the tremor rake her slender body as he brought her to climax, and absorbed her husky groan as he sent her up and over again.

She ran her hands over his shoulders, caressed the toned muscles, then slid to his hips and held him as she tore her mouth free and sought one male nipple with her mouth.

It wasn't fair that he should be in total control, except he didn't relinquish it for long. In one fluid movement he lifted her up against him and plunged deep inside, stilled briefly, then withdrew only to plunge again and again, increasing the strokes as her rhythm matched his and she held on as he took her for a shattering ride.

'Well, now,' Rafael murmured as his lips teased hers. 'That was some welcome home.'

He hadn't broken the intimate connection, and she shifted a little, raked her fingers through his hair, then held his head as she angled her mouth and took possession with a smooth slide of her tongue against his own.

'Greedy,' he accorded when he was able to speak, and she felt him harden deep inside.

This time it was she who set the pace, and it was achingly slow, with the soft slide of hands, the touch of lips, and the gentle rocking movement of two bodies in perfect tune.

It was a while before they indulged each other with a slow sensual lathering, then rinsed, they emerged to towel dry and slip into robes.

'Are you hungry?'

Rafael cast her a musing glance. 'I presume you're referring to food?' And delighted in the soft pink that coloured her cheeks.

'Of course.' She struggled to regain her composure. 'I put a casserole on a timer in the microwave. It won't take long to heat a baguette, and mix a salad.'

They fed each other, and it became a sensual feast as each mouthful became a promise of what would soon follow.

'I think I should go away more often,' Rafael drawled musingly.

Mikayla stood to her feet and began collecting plates.

'Leave them,' he instructed huskily, and pulled her down onto his lap. He nuzzled his mouth against the soft curve of her neck. 'I missed you.'

It was an admission of sorts, and one she took at face value. She hadn't liked being apart from him either. The large empty house, worse, an empty bed with no male warmth to sink into, no clever hands to tease and tantalise as emotions caught fire and burned.

She couldn't say the words, she was too afraid what he might read into them. Instead she cradled his face and initiated a soft kiss that lingered long before he rose to his feet with her in his arms and retraced his steps to the bedroom.

The loving was long and sweet, alternately tender and rawly primitive through the night, and they didn't emerge downstairs again until after midday.

It was then she thought to ask about his trip.

'Everything went well. Although I may have to fly to Brisbane for a few days later this month.' He smiled at the fleeting disappointment evident before she quickly masked it.

'I took Sammy out to dinner while you were away,' she said carefully.

'I imagine he was suitably impressed.'

A fleeting smile tugged the edges of her mouth. 'Yes. I also had Maisie stay overnight. I hope you don't mind.' Trivial stuff, but she couldn't think of anything scintillating to contribute.

'Why should I mind?'

The phone rang, and Rafael bit off a soft curse, then crossed to answer it.

Mikayla mixed eggs to make two omelettes, slid bread into the toaster, and organised coffee.

He ended the call just as she served the food onto the table.

'I'll have to put in a few hours in the study,' he relayed as he took a seat.

'That's okay. I've essays to mark, lessons to set for next week.'

They didn't go out from the house for the rest of the weekend, and it was infinitely relaxing to just *be*. They took time to watch a selection of videos, and while Rafael worked at the computer, she indulged herself by reading a latest mainstream release.

There was a degree of regret when the weekend came to a close, for Monday brought the routine of work, and the first of a number of social invitations spread over the ensuing few weeks.

There was a film première, an invitation-only showing at a prestigious art gallery, and cocktails hosted in honour of a visiting dignitary…at none of which Sasha put in an appearance.

Maybe she was out of town, Mikayla ruminated as she stood at Rafael's side in the lounge of a magnificent harbour-side villa where the evening's prestigious party was being held.

Mikayla recognised some of the guests, and found herself drawn into a conversation on the merits of the current scholastic system. It was a subject on which she held strong views, and she became engrossed with expressing detailed facts…to the degree she failed to notice Sasha's entrance until the discussion concluded.

'Rafael.'

Mikayla almost held her breath at the vision of perfection that was Sasha Despojoa and the almost-there gown moulding her perfectly curved slender frame. *Stunning* didn't quite cut it.

Rafael responded with practised charm, whilst Enrico projected cultivated charisma, and Mikayla could only wonder at the social games people were wont to play in a farce that hid dislike and jealousy.

'I trust your business trip went well, darling?' Sasha queried with a sultry smile filled with hidden promise as she touched a hand to Rafael's arm. 'Mikayla appeared not to miss you. Enrico and I caught her enjoying a clandestine dinner with a very handsome young man.' She shifted her gaze to Mikayla, and although she smiled, her eyes portrayed an icy venom as she waited for Rafael's reaction.

Mikayla caught his expression, saw the dark stillness in his eyes, the slightly raised eyebrow as he studied her thoughtfully.

She had no need to defend herself, and she didn't even try. 'Sammy D'alvecchio,' she relayed quietly, 'is a sixteen-year-old student who topped his class in a pre-exam test. The prize was a dinner date with me at a restaurant of my choice.' She paused fractionally, speared Sasha with a clear look, then aimed for the kill. 'There was no need to insult me, or Sammy for that matter, by leaving a message on the answering machine labelling him my toy-boy.'

'He looked at least twenty, darling,' Sasha protested with a contrived pout.

'So do a lot of sixteen-year-old students out of school uniform,' Mikayla rationalised.

'I think you're prevaricating,' Sasha opined, shrugging off Enrico's hand.

'Why would I do that?' Mikayla queried. 'You made a point of stopping by the table, and I performed an introduction.'

'Let it go, Sasha,' Enrico suggested sagely, and led her away.

'Sammy obviously looked his best,' Rafael drawled seconds later.

'Hardly recognisable,' Mikayla agreed, her gaze steady as he brushed light fingers down her cheek.

'Sasha needs to move on.'

'She doesn't want to give you up,' she declared wryly. 'Enrico is simply bait, and I'm expendable.'

His smile held sensual warmth, and a degree of humour. 'How do you feel about an early night?'

Her heart kicked against her ribs and quickened to a faster beat. 'How early?'

'Another hour, and we can leave without causing offence.'

'That soon?'

His soft laughter curled round her nerve-ends as he caught hold of her hand. 'Let's circulate, shall we?'

It was almost eleven when they thanked their host

and hostess, and slipped away from the glittering party.

The crisp cool air filled her lungs as they walked to the car, and it seemed no time at all before they reached neighbouring Woollahra and home.

Rafael hoisted her over one shoulder as they gained the foyer, and she aimed a playful fist to his ribs.

'Caveman tactics, huh?'

In the bedroom he lowered her down to her feet and kissed her with a thoroughness that sent heat flaring through her body. Clothes, his, hers, were abandoned with more speed than care, and he pulled her onto the bed without ceremony in a loving that was raw and primitive.

It became a passion that knew no bounds, and Mikayla met and matched it with a hunger of her own. There was no sense of time or place, just two people caught up in the throes of primeval desire.

Later, much later, they lay with limbs still entangled, lulled by the aftermath of mind-blowing sex.

Dear heaven, had it been the same for Rafael? Had he felt so completely consumed by emotions so tumultuous it resulted in total meltdown?

She couldn't think, and knew she couldn't move. At least not yet. *Sated* took on an entirely new meaning, the soothing brush of his fingers from shoulder to hip caused ripples of sensation over highly sensitised skin.

Gradually her breathing resumed its normal pattern, and her heartbeat slowed.

Rafael touched her temple with his lips, then slid

down to cover her mouth in a kiss that was so filled with evocative *tendresse* she almost cried.

It would be so easy to say *I love you*. She wanted to, badly. But, with the joy of knowing love, there came the knowledge that it would never be returned. For she merely represented payment of a debt in human kind.

Mikayla lay awake long after Rafael's breathing slowed and steadied, and she slipped from the bed, caught up a robe, and made her way quietly downstairs.

Moonlight filtered through the french doors overlooking the terrace, and she stood looking out over the darkened grounds, lost in contemplative thought.

Each day it became more difficult to stay, and as for the nights...how could she bear to continue to make love to a man who didn't love her? To occupy the same bed, accept such a degree of intimacy every night, and attempt to emotionally distance herself?

How was it possible to be uninvolved? To spend twelve more months with a man she loved with all her heart, then walk away?

It was bad enough now. In a year she doubted her ability to survive with her emotional sanity intact.

'Unable to sleep?'

The sound of Rafael's voice startled her, and her body trembled slightly as he curved his arms around her waist and he drew her back against him.

She desperately wanted to lean her head into his shoulder and absorb his strength.

'Mikayla?' Slowly he turned her round to face him.

She spread her hands. 'This...you, me, *us*,' she said wretchedly. 'When it ends, I'll move back into an apartment, resume my life.' *Without you*, she added silently, and felt part of her die inside.

His gaze narrowed. 'Does it necessarily have to end?' Dammit, he wanted her in his home, his bed. *His*.

He watched her features pale, those beautiful emerald eyes dilate and darken. 'How can it not?'

Every night was a vivid reminder of how difficult it would be to have to leave. There wasn't a time when she didn't agonise that each night they made love was one less night they'd share together.

He was everything. Her heart, her soul. No one else could come close.

'What if I were to ask you to stay?'

To continue in the role of mistress? Aware he might be tempted by another woman? Waiting, always waiting for the axe to fall when he would tell her to leave?

Mikayla knew she wouldn't be able to bear it. A hollow laugh rose and died in her throat. Dear Lord, even to think of it now was akin to having a lance pierce through her heart.

'For how long, Rafael?' she queried bravely. 'Until you tire of me?' And part acrimoniously? But how could they remain friends, but not lovers?

He reached out a hand and lay his palm to her cheek. 'Come back to bed.'

'Sex doesn't resolve anything.'

'To sleep, *querida*.' He slid an arm beneath her

knees, lifted her against his chest, then retraced his steps to the bedroom.

Now wasn't the time to tell her he had to take the midday flight to Brisbane, or that he'd be away several days on a business trip that would take him to Townsville and Cairns. The morning would be soon enough.

CHAPTER ELEVEN

RAFAEL walked off the plane, negotiated the concourse, collected his bag from the carousel, then signalled a cab.

It had been a long flight, a tense few days of heavy negotiations, and he was beat. He needed a shower, a long cool spritzer, and Mikayla...in that order.

The reverse, if truth be known, for once the deal had closed he'd chosen to take an earlier flight rather than wait until the next day.

Hell, he'd missed her slender toned body, the scent of her. He wanted to put his hands on her, watch as he brought her to orgasm, then take her hard and fast.

Afterwards he'd go the slow sensuous route, and ache at the husky sounds she made, delight in the arch of her body, the long slender neck as she tipped back her head and let him taste at will.

Dammit, his arousal was a primitive force, and he shifted in an effort to effect a measure of control.

At this time of night traffic was light, and the cab made good time through streets that were slick with recent rain.

He experienced impatient anticipation as he released the main gates for the cab to ascend the sweeping driveway. At the main entrance he pressed a note into the driver's hand and declined to wait for change.

The alarm system was on, but then he expected it to be. It was late, Mikayla was probably in bed, maybe even asleep.

A smile teased his lips at the thought of waking her as he climbed the stairs, doused the lights, and entered their bedroom.

Something was wrong. He could sense it, feel it, and he reached for the light switch, fear slamming through his body at the sight of the empty bed.

He checked the time. Maybe she was out, with a friend, Maisie…

It was then he caught sight of the envelope propped on the bedside pedestal.

He reached it in a few quick strides, tore the envelope open, and scanned the neatly written script.

The message was short, the words basic.

The clothes, gifts, everything he'd bought her reposed in drawers and the walk-in robe. The bank cheque attached to the written note was an added insult.

He went through an entire gamut of emotions… anger, frustration, cold hard rage. And had to admit he'd never felt so helpless in his life.

Dammit, it was *midnight*. The late hour didn't stop him from making a few phone calls, and he retraced his steps downstairs, entered the computer room and fired off a few urgent e-mail messages, pulled in a few favours.

It would be morning before he had any answers, and he poured himself a long cool spritzer, then when he'd drained the glass he took a leisurely hot shower and fell into bed.

Sleep was elusive, and he rose at dawn, pulled on a robe, took the first of a few calls, made a few more, had breakfast, checked the computer for incoming messages, then he dressed, slid behind the wheel of the Mercedes and eased the car out onto the street.

Mikayla hid a sigh of relief when the final bell rang signalling the end of class.

The day had started out bad with a flat tyre, she'd got caught in traffic and arrived late to school, and everything had gone steadily downhill from there.

Adding to it was her own increasing nervous tension as the day progressed. Anytime soon, Rafael would arrive home to an empty house and her note.

She gathered up her books, papers, and slid them into her satchel, then she emerged into the corridor, traversed it to the main entrance, and began walking towards the school car park.

'I'll carry your bag.'

The familiar teenage voice brought a smile, and she handed him her satchel. 'Thanks, Sammy.'

'Got something for you.' He thrust a hand into a trouser pocket, managed to look embarrassed, fierce, then as they drew further away from the buildings he pulled a small package out and handed it to her. 'It's nothing much. I just wanted you to have it.' He tried to scowl, and missed. 'For taking me to dinner.'

She was touched, and said so.

'Open it when you get home,' he said quickly.

She understood, and tucked it into her jacket pocket. 'Thank you. I'll treasure it.'

'Your boyfriend's here.'

Mikayla felt her heart stop as she caught sight of Rafael leaning indolently against the bonnet of his car.

He wasn't due back yet.

'You okay?'

Dammit, what could she say? 'Yes.'

'You two had an argument, or something?'

Or something. Her stomach knotted, and she had to consciously strive to keep her breathing even as she drew close.

Sammy was the first to speak. 'Hi, Rafael.'

Rafael spared him a smile. 'Sammy.'

'Good to see you again.'

Rafael inclined his head. 'Do me a favour,' he requested in a voice as smooth as silk, 'and walk. I need to talk to Mikayla alone.'

Sammy looked from one to the other, and settled on Mikayla's pale features. 'That okay with you?'

'It's fine.' It was anything but, and she caught Sammy's uncertainty before he turned and began retracing his steps.

'Get in the car, Mikayla.'

Dear heaven, he looked formidable. His features appeared cast from stone, and his eyes were so dark it hurt to meet his gaze.

'We've done this before.'

'Well, *hell*,' Rafael drawled. 'Let's do it again.'

She didn't want to see him alone. If he touched

her, she'd melt, and that would never do. Her chin tilted. 'I'll meet you at the café in Double Bay where we first shared coffee.'

He wanted to wring her slender neck. Instead, he inclined his head in silent acquiescence and slid in behind the wheel of his car.

Traffic was heavy, and it took longer than usual to reach the elite suburb, even longer to find a free parking space.

She had to walk a block and a half, and he was waiting for her, his gaze intent as she drew close.

'Coffee, or a cool drink?'

Mikayla took the chair he held out and sank down into it. 'A latte, thanks.'

He summoned a waiter, gave their order, then he folded his length into the chair opposite.

Take control. 'You read my note.'

He tamped down the anger. 'Did you really think you could run and hide, Mikayla?' he relayed with dangerous softness.

'If I wanted to hide, I'd be interstate using an assumed name.'

The waiter delivered their order, and she picked up two sugar tubes, broke them, and sprinkled the white granules on top of the froth.

He leaned back in his chair and regarded her carefully. 'You would willingly throw away what we share together?'

'Sex?'

One eyebrow slanted. 'Shall we start over? This time, no verbal games.'

'I don't know what you mean.'

'Yes,' he countered with indolent ease. 'You do. Explain why you felt compelled to leave.'

'This isn't a court of law.'

He inclined his head, and his faint smile held an edge of mockery. 'You know me well enough to understand I will insist you give me an answer.'

'I don't have the time. I'm due to begin work in half an hour.'

His eyes hardened. 'No,' he refuted silkily.

Mikayla had had enough. In one fluid movement she stood to her feet. 'Another night with you would have killed me.' Her eyes flashed green fire. 'Because fool that I am and, as hard as I tried not to…I fell in love with you.' Dear God, don't let me cry! 'You wanted a reason? You've got it.'

Without a further word she turned and fled, racing quickly between traffic, taking a short cut through a narrow lane before darting down another street to her car.

She fired the engine and drove away as if the devil himself was in pursuit.

Twenty minutes later she parked the Mini and entered the restaurant, greeted her employer, donned an apron and began setting tables.

It was a hell of a night. Busy, with patrons demanding faster service, complaining when she delivered herb instead of garlic bread, and she mixed up two orders, which earned her a stream of abuse.

Focus, concentrate, she bade repeatedly as she did

her best to please, with a smile that became increasingly strained as the evening wore on.

Worse, her employer seemed to think an eleven o'clock finish meant she stayed over time without pay, and at eleven thirty she walked into the kitchen, removed her apron, and left.

Twenty minutes later she drove down the side of the house she shared, and almost groaned out loud at the noise emitting from the house next door. A party?

She needed a shower, and bed. In peace and quiet. It didn't look as if she was going to get either.

The shower eased some of the tension, and it was only as she tidied her clothes that she remembered sliding Sammy's gift into her jacket pocket.

Mikayla removed it and carefully undid the wrapping. Inside a small square box reposed an exquisite crystal rosebud on a slender gold stem.

Emotion clouded her eyes as she attached it to the lapel of her jacket. Tomorrow he would see it there, and know how much the gift meant to her.

She was so tired she should have slept the instant her head hit the pillow. Instead she lay tossing and turning until the digital clock showed three, then she woke at seven, dressed, entered the communal kitchen, quickly ate cereal and fruit, followed it with coffee, then caught up her satchel and went out to her car.

Somehow she managed to get through the day, and she was never more thankful when the last class filed out and she was able to leave.

She could retreat to the common-room and begin

marking work there, but instead she decided to drive down to the nearest bay, park, and sit in the shade of a tree and breathe in some fresh air.

The sun hurt her eyes as she emerged from the main entrance, and she retrieved sunglasses, slid them on, and began walking towards the school's car park. Two students offered a greeting, a fellow teacher inclined 'have a good weekend', and it wasn't until she reached the reserved parking bay that she realised her Mini was nowhere in sight.

What on earth—?

In its place stood a silver Mercedes, and even as she assimilated its familiarity the door opened and Rafael slid to his feet.

'Where's the Mini?' she demanded heatedly.

'Parked in my garage.'

Anger rose like a red tide. 'You have no right—'

'Get in the car, Mikayla.'

'I'm damned if I will!'

'I have no particular aversion to causing a scene,' Rafael relayed hardily. 'Ten seconds.'

She opted for dignity, and chose total silence, not even offering him so much as a surreptitious glance during the drive to his Woollahra home.

There, as the automatic garage doors rose high, stood her Mini, and she released the door-clasp the instant his car slid to a halt beside it.

'Let's take this inside, shall we?'

'I don't have time—'

'I'll make it easy for you,' Rafael intercepted silkily as the doors rolled smoothly down. 'Your job at the restaurant no longer exists.'

'You found out where I work, and—' She was momentarily speechless. 'You can't do that!'

'It's done.' He crossed to the door leading into the house, and freed the lock.

'I hate you!'

He threw her a wry smile. 'At this precise moment, I guess you do.'

She wanted to *hit* him, and probably would, given the opportunity. Her eyes narrowed as he moved to the rear of the Mercedes, popped the trunk, and retrieved two bags and a box of books. *Hers.*

'How did you know—?'

One eyebrow slanted. 'Where you escaped to? I would think it's obvious.'

All it would take would be a few phone calls, the help of a private investigator. That wasn't the part that angered her. Going to the house she shared, entering her locked room under whatever plausible guise he'd used, did.

Mikayla drew a deep steadying breath in an effort to minimise her rage and indicated her bags. 'You can put those in the Mini.'

'That isn't the way it's going to happen.'

'The *hell* it isn't!' She flew at him and railed her fists against his chest, his shoulders, anywhere she could connect. Then skill kicked in and she got sneaky...to no avail, for he blocked each and every move, and stilled any further attempts by lifting her over one shoulder and anchoring her there as he strode into the house.

'Put me *down*!'

She held on with one hand and aimed for a vulnerable part of his anatomy with the other, only to have her hand caught in a crushing grip.

'Foul, *pequeña*.'

'What the hell is it *you're* doing?' she thrust furiously as he crossed the foyer and entered his study.

He closed the door, and she heard the lock snick into place as he lowered her down onto her feet.

'You're locking us *in*?'

'For the moment.'

She threw him a fulminating glare as she straightened her skirt and smoothed a hand over her hair. 'I could have you up for abduction!'

'Try it.'

'I demand you hand me the keys to my car and let me go.'

'No.'

His indomitable will was the final straw.

'*Why?*' It was a cry from the heart, and she fought to still the hot angry tears threatening to spill. 'Damn you. What more do you want from me than you haven't already had?'

It got to him in a way nothing else had, and he pushed her gently into a chair and moved a few feet to rest one hip against the edge of his desk.

'*You,*' he revealed quietly. 'Just—you.'

A haunted look sharpened her features and deepened the colour of her eyes.

He wanted to *shake* her. 'Did you sleep at all last night?'

Her shoulders lifted in a helpless shrug. 'Some.'

'At a guess, you missed lunch.'

He couldn't know for sure, and she had no intention of telling him he was right.

'Rafael—'

'Did you think you could make a statement like *I fell in love with you,* and walk away?' he demanded with chilling softness.

'You wanted a reason why I left,' she said with a bravado she didn't feel. 'I gave you one.'

'And then you ran.'

'What did you expect me to do, Rafael? Stay, and be totally humiliated by your amusement?' Helpless anger surged through her body, tinging her cheeks a deep pink and lending her eyes a dangerous green fire. 'Do you have any idea what it cost me to tell you? *Do you?*' she demanded fiercely. *'You,'* she verbally stabbed. 'The hardened self-sufficient entrepreneur, who has total control of his emotions.' She stood to her feet. 'And me, the sexual innocent. I didn't stand a chance, did I?' She was on a roll. 'I thought I could take a year out of my life, play the mistress role, then walk away.' A self-derisory laugh choked in her throat. 'Emotions intact, heart-whole.' What a fool.

His gaze never left hers for a second. 'What made you think I'd humiliate you?' He paused fractionally. 'Or be amused?'

'You can have any woman you want. Sasha merely

heads a queue of willing females eager to leap into your bed. I was—'

'An amusing diversion?'

'*Yes.*'

'Whom I could easily shrug off without a second thought?' He didn't give her a chance to answer. 'That's why I worked half the night to finish negotiations in order to catch an early flight home?'

'The sex is good.'

He barely restrained himself from hauling her into his arms, clearing the desk, and showing her just how good it could be. 'But any woman will do?'

'I imagine so.'

'*Por Dios.*' There was nothing pious about the way the words emerged, and her eyes widened measurably at his vicious tone. 'What manner of man do you think I am?'

She couldn't answer him, and a muscle tensed at the edge of his jaw.

'I won't deny a degree of revenge and a need for justice influenced me to take up your sacrificial offer, conditional on every protective legality in my favour.'

He paused, subjecting her features to an encompassing appraisal, and a wry smile tugged the edges of his mouth.

'I soon discovered just how sacrificial,' he recalled, remembering her innocence. 'With every action you forced me to reassess my original judgement. Strength, pride...you possessed both. And as you say, the sex was good.

'But it was more than that,' he continued, his dark

eyes still, contemplative. 'Much more. For both of us.'

Mikayla sat, almost afraid to move. The room was quiet, so quiet, and she couldn't have looked away from him if she'd tried.

'Sasha—'

'Sasha is—*was*,' he corrected with quiet savagery, 'a pleasant companion who wanted a permanent relationship,' he enlightened wryly. 'I didn't. End of story.'

Without a further word he reached across his desk, retrieved a document and thrust it into her hands. 'Read it.'

She looked at it, then shifted her gaze to fuse with his.

'Just—read it, Mikayla,' Rafael instructed with hard inflexibility.

It contained less than two pages, and the legal clauses were crystal clear. Signed by Rafael Velez-Aguilera and witnessed by his lawyer. Voiding the original agreement agreed to and signed by Rafael Velez-Aguilera and Mikayla Petersen. And exonerating Mikayla Petersen from all debt incurred by Joshua Petersen.

'*Why?*' It was a cry from the heart.

'Because I don't want anything to stand between us.'

She should have been relieved beyond relief. Instead she felt incredibly empty.

'You had no need to do this,' she said shakily. 'I would have paid you back every cent.'

'Your honesty isn't in question.' He eased himself away from the desk and took a step towards her. 'You refused to take money from me. Even in New York, you didn't touch a single note of the amount I left at your disposal in the safe. Clothes were restricted to minimal purchases. And you left them all behind.' He thrust hands into his trouser pockets. 'Together with a bank cheque for most of the salary you'd earned during the past three months.'

'It represented an instalment on the money owed you.'

'I've counter-signed the cheque and banked it in your name.' He restrained his anger with difficulty. 'Do you have any idea what it felt like to walk into this house and find you gone? *Do you?*' He swore briefly, pithily. 'Thank your God it was past midnight, and I had no way of discovering where you were until daylight.'

Mikayla didn't say a word. Her breath seemed locked in her throat, and she watched as he lifted a hand and raked fingers through his hair, ruffling it into attractive disorder.

'Any sooner, and I think I would have killed you,' he relayed with quiet savagery.

The phone rang, and he cast it an irritated glance, then he picked up the receiver, intoned a few brief words, listened, concurred, then he ended the call and raked her slender frame.

She looked as fragile as delicate Venetian glass, and he was afraid if he touched her she'd shatter.

He offered her a slow smile, and she remained hesitant as he linked her hand in his and brought it to his lips.

She felt as jittery as a teenager on her first date, and the feeling was so ridiculous as to be laughable. She'd lived with the man for three months, slept with him, shared riveting, mind-blowing sex…why should she be nervous, for heaven's sake?

'Do you trust me?'

'Rafael—'

He pressed a finger against her lips. 'It's simple. Just answer *yes* or *no*.'

It could only be one. 'Yes,' she evinced slowly.

'There's something I need to ask you.'

Please don't ask me to continue being your mistress, she begged silently. I don't think I could bear it.

'Marry me.'

Mikayla heard the words, and found it difficult to assimilate them. 'You can't be serious?'

He was, utterly. She could see evidence of it in his features, the darkness of his eyes. There was purpose, commitment, and something else she was almost afraid to define.

Emotion rose from deep within, until it became too much to control, and her eyes filled with unshed tears.

'Madre de Dios,' Rafael swore softly. 'Don't cry.'

'I'm not.' And knew she lied, for twin rivulets of moisture rolled slowly down each cheek, and she brushed at them impatiently.

She lifted her head and looked at him through a

watery mist, then she offered a shaky smile as he trailed fingers along the edge of her jaw.

'I love you.' He fastened his mouth over hers in a kiss that was so incredibly gentle, it was all she could do to hold the tears at bay.

'You have my heart, my soul. *Yours*, for the rest of my life.' He swept an arm beneath her knees and carried her upstairs. When they reached the bedroom he let her slide down to her feet and caged her close.

Dear God, this felt good. So good. His warmth, his scent… it was like coming home after riding a storm.

'How do you feel about Paris?'

Mikayla wrapped her arms round his waist. 'I've always wanted to go there.'

He smiled over the top of her head, and thought of the two airline tickets in his desk drawer. 'A small intimate wedding?'

'Just a few close friends.'

He waited a beat. 'Sunday.'

She went still. 'Which Sunday?'

'This weekend, *querida*.'

'But we can't—'

'Yes,' he drawled. 'We can.' He didn't give her time to think. 'I've booked the Celebrant, the caterers, and we're due to board a flight to France on Monday.'

She lifted her head, saw the deep emotion evident, and could only echo weakly, 'Sunday?'

His mouth touched hers, and this time there was passion as his tongue slid in to tangle with hers.

'Do you object?'

Mikayla wound her arms up round his neck. 'No.'

Rafael freed the buttons on her blouse and eased it from her shoulders as he nibbled the soft scented curve at the edge of her neck. 'You've forgotten something,' he said gently.

Her own fingers were busy as she began on his shirt buttons.

'What's that?'

Her bra fell to the floor and his hands skimmed low over her hips.

'You haven't said yes.'

She attacked his belt, undid his trousers, then slid her hands beneath the silk covering his buttocks.

'Hmn.' She pretended to consider, teasing him, then gave a groan in capitulation as his teeth grazed the sensitive hollow at the base of her neck. *'Yes.'*

He trailed his mouth lower and hovered over the hardened peak of her breast. 'I should punish you for that.' And proceeded to suckle until she begged for mercy.

'I've organised for you to take two weeks compassionate leave from school.'

Her fingers stilled momentarily. 'You have?'

The silken briefs followed his trousers, and he caught back a groan as she reached for him.

'Thoughtful of you.' Her hand slid low and she cupped him, squeezing gently, then trailed her fingers over his appendage, smiling secretively at his indrawn breath.

Then it was her turn to gasp as he sought the apex between her thighs, skilfully stroked her, and caught her gasp with his mouth as she went up and over.

Just as she recovered, he sent her up again, and this time she gave a husky growl and drew him down onto the bed.

It was fast, almost as if they couldn't get enough of each other, then when they had time to catch their breath they indulged in a slow sweet loving, their bodies arching gently, and soft moans silvered the air as sensual pleasure replaced heated passion.

Sunday dawned a beautiful day, the sun shone brightly and there was just a drift of cloud in the sky.

Maisie and Sammy stood with Rafael's lawyer as the Celebrant conducted the marriage ceremony.

Mikayla had chosen an ivory silk suit, matching pumps, and she wore a fashionable wide-brimmed hat with ribboned roses.

Rafael looked resplendent in a dark three-piece suit, and they exchanged vows with solemn dedication.

Except for Mikayla, whose voice shook slightly after Rafael slid a circlet of diamonds on her finger and followed it with a magnificent pear-shaped diamond engagement ring.

Afterwards the few guests indulged in fine food and superb champagne on the lawn, then when the sun set in a glorious slow slide of rich golds, deep rose and purple, the guests departed and Rafael swept an arm beneath Mikayla's knees and carried her into the house.

He removed her hat, then kissed her so thoroughly her head swam.

The buzz of the intercom intruded, and Rafael reluctantly released her.

'That will be the limousine.' He pressed his mouth to hers, briefly, then straightened. 'I'll fetch our bags from the study.'

The hotel suite was magnificent, situated on a high floor with panoramic views over the harbour.

Mikayla turned towards Rafael and saw the warmth evident, the heat, the passion, and her lips curved into a wicked smile.

'Do we get to eat dinner?'

'Later.'

'Room service?' A soft chuckle emerged from her throat. 'Eventually?' she teased as he moved towards her.

'Are you hungry?'

She wound her arms up round his neck and pulled his face down to hers. 'Only for you.' She leaned into him, felt the pulse of his body against her own, and sought his mouth in an evocative lingering kiss. 'Always, only you.'

Rafael cupped her face with his hands, and she nearly died at the wealth of emotion evident. 'You're my life. My love.' He brushed his lips against the slightly swollen contours of her own, savoured, then lifted fractionally. 'Everything.'

**Lindsay Armstrong...
Helen Bianchin...
Emma Darcy...
Miranda Lee...**

Some of our bestselling writers are Australians!

Look out for their novels about the Wonder from Down Under—where spirited women win the hearts of Australia's most eligible men.

THE AUSTRALIANS

Coming soon:
A QUESTION OF MARRIAGE
by Lindsay Armstrong
On sale October 2001, Harlequin Presents® #2208

And look out for:
FUGITIVE BRIDE
by Miranda Lee
On sale November 2001, Harlequin Presents® #2212

Available wherever Harlequin books are sold.

HARLEQUIN®
Makes any time special ®

Visit us at www.eHarlequin.com   HPSEAUS

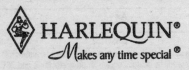

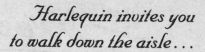

Harlequin invites you to walk down the aisle...

To honor our year long celebration of weddings, we are offering an exciting opportunity for you to own the Harlequin Bride Doll. Handcrafted in fine bisque porcelain, the wedding doll is dressed for her wedding day in a cream satin gown accented by lace trim. She carries an exquisite traditional bridal bouquet and wears a cathedral-length dotted Swiss veil. Embroidered flowers cascade down her lace overskirt to the scalloped hemline; underneath all is a multi-layered crinoline.

Join us in our celebration of weddings by sending away for your own Harlequin Bride Doll. This doll regularly retails for $74.95 U.S./approx. $108.68 CDN. One doll per household. Requests must be received no later than December 31, 2001. Offer good while quantities of gifts last. Please allow 6-8 weeks for delivery. Offer good in the U.S. and Canada only. Become part of this exciting offer!

Simply complete the order form and mail to:
"A Walk Down the Aisle"

<table>
<tr><td>

IN U.S.A
P.O. Box 9057
3010 Walden Ave.
Buffalo, NY 14269-9057
</td><td>

IN CANADA
P.O. Box 622
Fort Erie, Ontario
L2A 5X3
</td></tr>
</table>

Enclosed are eight (8) proofs of purchase found in the last pages of every specially marked Harlequin series book and $3.75 check or money order (for postage and handling). Please send my Harlequin Bride Doll to:

_____

Name (PLEASE PRINT)

_____

Address   Apt. #

_____

City   State/Prov.   Zip/Postal Code

_____

Account # (if applicable)   **097 KIK DAEW**

HARLEQUIN®
Makes any time special ®

Visit us at www.eHarlequin.com

A Walk Down the Aisle
Free Bride Doll Offer
One Proof-of-Purchase

PHWDAPOPR2

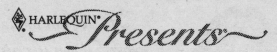

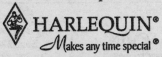